"Talk about luck!" Molly chortled. She backed up a pace. "They're coming this way! The guys, I mean! Quick, Suzy, invent something clever to say!"

My brain obligingly cranked out a couple of bright words and sat them on my tongue. I focused on those faces.

The first face was your typical American male structure. Brown hair, a square jawline, pale freckles dotting the arch of a blunt-tipped nose.

My gaze shifted to the other one. I caught full force the smiling face of Kevin Dowling.

Kevin Dowling! The "mysterious young stranger" in Days of Loving! Here in Hillsboro!

I heard only dimly the crash of ceramic as the dish of coleslaw slipped past my fingers and splatted against the cement walk.

Dear Readers:

Thank you for your unflagging interest in First Love From Silhouette. Your many helpful letters have shown us that you have appreciated growing and stretching with us, and that you demand more from your reading than happy endings and conventional love stories. In the months to come we will make sure that our stories go on providing the variety you have come to expect from us. We think you will enjoy our unusual plot twists and unpredictable characters who will surprise and delight you without straying too far from the concerns that are very much part of all our daily lives.

We hope you will continue to share with us your ideas about how to keep our books your very First Loves. We depend on you to keep us on our toes!

Nancy Jackson
Senior Editor
FIRST LOVE FROM SILHOUETTE

DAYS
OF LOVING
Jean F. Capron

First Love from Silhouette

Published by Silhouette Books New York

America's Publisher of Contemporary Romance

To the Capron Seven,
They Know Who They Are

SILHOUETTE BOOKS
300 E. 42nd St., New York, N.Y. 10017

ISBN: 0-373-06218-4

First Silhouette Books printing January 1987

America's Publisher of Contemporary Romance

Printed in the U.S.A.

RL 6.5, IL age 11 and up

JEAN F. CAPRON grew up in New Jersey, and at one time she, her husband and their seven children ran a dairy farm. "Everyone on the premises participated, willingly or not," she says. When her children reached school age, she enrolled in a creative writing course. She is the author of four previous novels and a string of magazine short stories. She lives in a small town in New York state, where she writes a weekly column for the local newspaper.

Chapter One

My intent was to snooze as late as possible Monday morning, not even bothering to get up for breakfast. After all, it was the end of June...school vacation.

"Suzy, up and at 'em!" My mother's voice reached in and shook the life from a really top-flight dream. She snapped loose the bedroom window shade. Sunlight streamed in, laying warm fingers on my eyelids.

"You promised to help me pick and shell the garden peas," she reminded me.

Sometimes, in a rash moment, I promise some pretty weird things. And then, later, when the head clears...

"Up, up, up!" She snatched away my sheet. A losing battle. The only comfort was the aroma of the sizzling bacon that drifted from below.

My philosophy was, if one must indulge in backbreaking labor, one might just as well do it on a full stomach. Naturally I grumbled all through breakfast and the dishes that followed. I grumbled even louder when my kid brother, who has two perfectly capable hands and plenty of energy, turned out to be missing. Danny had, as usual, taken off on his ten-speed, leaving only little me to pick and shell.

Mom shrugged and smiled. "Well, that's Danny for you," she said. "Always off exploring new horizons."

Ha-ha, funny. But then there was very little about my twelve-year-old brother that I found amusing.

Kneeling among the vines, I reached for fat green pods, yanked and deposited them in my pail, keeping up a rough rhythm until halfway through the first row. The midmorning sun had gathered steam and was moving in for the kill. I creaked to my haunches and took a swipe at the sweat dribbling down my face.

Mom, who freezes peas religiously every summer and ignores such petty annoyances, was still at it, yanking and depositing with a speed I had absolutely no desire to imitate. I glanced furtively about, yearning for distraction.

Molly Fancher, who has been hanging out with me for years, loomed into view. She eased past the carrots and beets and settled in next to the lettuce, but away from the peas, lest I accidentally con her into assisting.

Molly was sixteen, and I was fifteen. She was four months older than I, and never let me forget it.

"What's new?"

"Oh, nothing." Molly rocked back and forth on her heels. "At least nothing I'd care to mention."

"Molly!" From my mother, who actually paused in her labors to greet Molly with enthusiasm. "What's this I hear about your father..."

"...remarrying?" Molly's long, pointy face clouded. She took a couple of breaths that sounded pretty raspy to me. "I can't deny it, Mrs. Jensen." She sank to her rump in the lettuce, squashing at least two leafy budding heads. Not that she noticed.

I should explain, at this point, that Molly's parents were divorced the year she was seven, which is why this scrawny, asthmatic little kid came from Chicago to start second grade with me at Hillsboro Middle School. She and her mother lived right around the corner from us, on Floyd Avenue, in the bungalow-type green-shingled house in which Mrs. Fancher had grown up. Just the two of them, finally, Molly's grandparents having died off before she turned thirteen. Her mother worked as receptionist for our dentist, Dr. Oswald, three days a week.

Way back when, Mom and Dad and Mr. and Mrs. Fancher had attended Hillsboro High together. They were pretty good friends. I think Mom considered Adam Fancher a nice enough person. "Decent," she

called him once. Apparently the divorce was nobody's fault; their marriage just hadn't worked out.

"Ah, yes," Molly muttered to me, "how good news
does get around. Daddy-O is definitely taking the
plunge again."

"So where's the tragedy?" I asked her. "It won't
change things between your father and you. You'll still
be with him on Thanksgivings and Easters and spend
the summers with him."

A thick-throated sound erupted from Molly.
"Summers?" If I hadn't known better I'd have sworn
she was about to explode into an asthma attack. Molly
hasn't had a bad attack in years.

Mom glanced up from the peas. "Gladys told me,
just the other day; she was picking up your flight res-
ervation for Chicago, so you'll be there in plenty of
time for the wedding."

Molly whipped a bronchi-nasal dilator from her
jeans pocket. She took a long ragged draft of it.

"You are going to the wedding—aren't you?" I
asked.

"Guess again," she said.

"No wedding?"

"And no summer." She fingered the dilator.
"Seems his bride-to-be suddenly decided to keep the
wedding list small. Like, the two of the them, plus a
couple of unnamed witnesses. And I didn't need an ax
to fall on me to get the drift that I'd be as welcome as
the plague this summer."

"Your father said that?"

"Oh, they were polite about it. Said something about later, maybe August, after they'd had time to catch their breaths. But I got the message, all right."

From the corner of my eye I could see Mom open her mouth, then close it into a tight line. She made a grab for some vines. She didn't even look up when I quit at the end of my row, and Molly and I took off for the front porch.

Molly and I had spent every fall, winter, spring and summer knocking around together. We'd weathered such horrors as basic algebra, home economics and Mrs. Bandy's fourth-period gym class, without killing each other. We'd probably spend this summer doing the same.

The prospects for a lively summer looked pretty dim. Aside from the fact that Molly and I sometimes grate on each other's nerves after prolonged exposure, most summers in Hillsboro do bog down. There's swimming at the municipal pool, except for the first week in August, when they drain, clean and refill. There's our downtown movie, the Bijou, and the drive-in one on the outskirts, and the bowling alleys and the tennis courts and the roller rink—plus Firemen's Field Day, the end of July. Stuff like that. As for our social life: Molly had been dating Mike Edwards all spring. He'd doubtless be hanging around her. And Jimmy Wingate, a fixture in my growing-up life, would be underfoot if I but wiggled my pinkie finger. Ho hum....

We positioned ourselves on the top porch step. I let my gaze roam the length of Meridian Street. Not much was stirring, not even a breeze.

And least of all Molly Fancher. She was slumped forward, her shoulder wings protruding, her hands dangling between jeaned knees, her eyes heavy lidded and hound-dog. I don't know how she does that. I mean, manage to look so lone and lost so easily. It's a talent.

"We could work our way to Hamburger Heaven and split a double-decker," I ventured, needing to hear the sound of a human voice. "I can dig up a dollar's change if you can."

"Forget it!"

Sometimes that girl . . . Oh well.

Another try. "I suppose we could drag in and turn on the TV. The picture's a little dim, and everything's game shows right now because that's what's on mornings. Afternoons, my mother watches soap operas. Ever catch any, Molly?"

A grunt came from her depths, which you could interpret any way you wanted. She whipped out the nasal dilator.

"I only watch them for laughs myself. I mean, isn't it hilarious the way people get hooked on those dumb things? How anybody can focus on them day in and day out... Although there is one at three o'clock, *Days of Loving*, that's at least bearable. Not that I follow it, exactly, but it's on when I get home from school and all summer long, so I'm stuck. And some of its

characters... oh, like, take this guy, Kevin Dowling,
for instance. He's a newcomer to Locust Point. You
might call him a 'mysterious young stranger.' As soon
as he shows, dire things begin to happen. Like, a town
old-timer's found murdered, his corpse is stuffed in an
abandoned fireplace, the local bank is burgled, Jessica Morgan, daughter of Locust Point's beloved Dr.
Jim, disappears shortly after dating Kevin. Who, by
the way, is an absolute *doll*. I mean you just know he's
no murderer or bad guy; somebody has to be framing
him. Anyway... Kevin also disappears, and Dr. Jim's
son, Josh, who happens to be a police detective, is
nosing out some promising leads. But... Molly? Are
you still in this world?''

It's no cinch trying to converse with a raspy-
breathed sphinx.

"Dad's due back from Arizona tonight," I suddenly remembered. "Guess I'd better make myself
useful around here." My father's a field representa-
tive for a Fleet City manufacturing outfit, and he
travels a lot. That week he'd been in Tucson, scaring
up stainless-steel-gasket sales. "You know how moth-
ers get about having everything neat and cozy before
the warriors come home from the front. My dad—"

Molly's eyes swiveled, caught mine and threatened
homicide.

Some days I can't do anything right. It seemed almost a relief to spot my mother hauling into view,
armed with two pails of peas to be shelled.

Conversation settled into busy-fingered silence while Mom and I emptied pods and Molly sat there, watching. Molly had developed a real knack for watching. I'd shelled about a third of mine, when Mom slackened off long enough to say something.

Actually, what loosened her tongue was the long, sleek blue Buick that slowed before the MacAllister house across the street. Mr. and Mrs. MacAllister had gone to Beaumont, Texas, for three months, to visit their daughter. "Rumor has it," Mom confided, "they're renting it out for the summer to a family from New York City."

A chubby middle-aged couple got out and marched up the MacAllister front walk. Behind them plodded two young-male types hugging suitcases.

"Not too bad," Molly reported, her eyes creasing at the corners. She slid the dilator into her jeans pocket. "If you go for tall, masculine and neatly filled out."

I combed green-stained fingers through my straggly mouse-brown locks and hoped for a miracle if they were to turn around.

"I suppose it would be neighborly," Mom said, gazing after them, "if I contributed a little something to help tide them over. At least until they're settled."

People in Hillsboro often did that for newcomers. It's our peculiar style of welcoming. I pictured her whipping together the meat loaf, coleslaw and zucchini bread that had made her name a household word at church picnics and Meridian Street block parties.

"Still...people from New York City..." My mother was experiencing second thoughts.

Molly stayed for lunch. The morning's arrivals had lifted her mood and done wonders for her tongue. Between slurps of chicken soup and gulped-down bologna sandwich, she managed, with her usual skill, to maneuver discussion to the new neighbors. "I," she announced, "intend to get a closer look. With or without you." She aimed her soup spoon at me, as if meaning to shoot down any possible objection.

Who was objecting?

There were still a few peas to be shelled. To appear as if she were an authentic part of our scenery, Molly actually went to work on them. Her fingers don't take naturally to popping and shelling. After a bumbling try she slowed from poke-along to complete stop, while she surveyed the across-street terrain for movement.

As if to accommodate her, the boys wandered outside and began setting up a badminton net between two saplings, then launched into action. From where we sat they looked like tall, muscled anybodies in cut-off shorts, halfheartedly batting around a shuttlecock.

"This will never do," Molly said. "If we're ever to meet them, we'll have to make up some reasonable excuse."

Behind us the door creaked open. "Girls," my mother said, "would it gum up your routine if I asked you to deliver—'' She thrust forward a ceramic bowl of her famed coleslaw.

I cluthched the bowl with suddenly numb fingers.

"Just rap at their door and explain that it's a little house-warmer from the neighbors. Or use your own words, Suzy. I trust you to say the right thing."

We set off at a brisk pace.

"Talk about luck," Molly chortled, steering me in the right direction. "First we'll go to the door and unload the slaw, then we'll just happen to . . . uh-oh!" She backed up a pace. "They're coming this way! The guys, I mean. Quickly, Suzy, invent something clever to say! Don't let me down . . . !"

My brain obligingly cranked out a bunch of bright words and sat them on my tongue. I focused on those faces. The words shriveled like dew in the a.m. sun.

The first face was your typical American-male structure: lots of dark brown hair, a square jawline, pale freckles dotting the arch of a blunt-tipped nose. Alert brown eyes. A wide mouth that curved easily into a grin.

My gaze shifted to the other one and caught, full force, the smiling face of Kevin Dowling.

The Mysterious Young Stranger, here, in Hillsboro?

I heard, only dimly, the crash of ceramic, as the coleslaw slipped past my fingers and splatted against the MacAllister cement walk.

Chapter Two

Mom was more silent than usual during the evening meal. For one thing, the bowl had been her favorite. And I can't deny that it had been a humiliating experience, spending a half hour on our knees, scraping coleslaw from the MacAllister front walk, with a token assist from the two boys and the grudging help of Molly Fancher.

Danny was carefully plucking onion strips from his steak and depositing them in neat rows along the plate edge. Onions top his picky no-no list, closely followed by mushrooms, beets, turnips and cauliflower. He glanced over at Mom, apparently expecting her usual lecture on wasting perfectly good food. But she kept on slicing and munching, as if her mind was working on something else.

I believe in conversation at the table. Especially when I have a point to make. "I don't care what anybody says," I said abruptly, "I *know* that was Kevin Dowling!" So there.

Mom put down her fork. "Suzanne, need I remind you, Kevin is a fictional character on a soap opera? His disappearance from Locust Point means only that the actor playing the part is probably on vacation. Never fear, in about three weeks he'll resurface, tanned and rested."

"Speaking of mysterious strangers," Danny volunteered past a mouthful of dill pickle, "there's a slew of them down by the Stokes place. I was exploring for buried treasure, y'know, and these guys were swarming all over the house. There was this big old van and a couple of camper trucks and a fancy black car, like a hearse limo almost . . ."

The kid certainly did know how to draw attention.

"Well, gee," he said plaintively, upon being cornered, "how would I know what they were up to?" He brightened. "Hey, maybe making a movie or something. Because there were all these cameras and guys dragging furniture and flowerpots and what looked like walls."

"Nobody's been inside that house since Leonard Stokes died last winter," Mom said, looking thoughtful.

The way the town grapevine had it, Mr. Stokes's son, Barney, had been gone from Hillsboro for years. The talk was, there'd been bad blood between father and son, and Barney had left home, vowing never to return. They did say he'd slipped into town to make funeral arrangements for his father, but I guess he must have slipped out immediately afterward, because nobody'd had the chance to speak to him. Barney had graduated from high school with Mom and Dad. His name cropped up occasionally in their conversation. I was just about to ask a few pertinent questions when the phone rang.

Jimmy Wingate had picked that moment to call. I caught up with him on the second ring. "Suzy?" He sounded out of breath and slightly hoarse, as if he'd been running or jumping up and down and shouting. "Guess what?"

"You *got* it."

"Ye-a-ah." I could almost reach out and touch the satisfaction oozing through his voice. Jimmy's junior driving license had finally arrived. He'd been awaiting it for days, driving us all mucho loco with his talking about it.

"Hallelujah!"

"My sentiments exactly." Pause. "Suzy, remember what you said you'd do when I got my license?"

"Uh, yes. But . . ."

"You promised, and I'm holding you to it. My father lent me the shekels for the auto insurance, so the Chevette's all set. New slipcovers on the bucket seats, cherry red, just as you suggested; engine's tuned, fresh spark plugs, reconditioned interior, AM-FM radio, exterior paint job, recapped whitewalls..."

I could picture Jimmy ticking off the improvements he'd paid for with his own money saved up from the part-time job at his Uncle Steve's Superette.

"You and me and Camille. Of course Camille will sit behind us—"

"And her fleas will ride along with her, she'll scratch and make that funny whining noise and lick off the back of my neck...."

"No problem. I just bought her a new flea collar, and she's been warned to be on her good behavior. See ya in fifteen minutes." Click.

My mother wasted no time in taking over the phone. "Gladys?" Pause. "Say, Gladys, I wonder if you've heard what I heard about the Stokes place. It seems that—what? Yes, a van, two campers, and a—you heard *what*?" Spotting me, she covered the phone's mouthpiece. "Shut the door behind you, Suzy," she said. "And try to get back early. In time to put away the dishes. You were saying, Gladys...?"

Jimmy and his Chevette arrived shortly after, Camille in the back seat, sitting up straight and regal, like a scruffy queen on her throne. When Jimmy got out the queen dissolved into a familiar tail-wagging lively-old-lady mongrel who would hop to her master's every command as she'd been doing since he'd been a little kid.

I've always liked the looks of Jimmy Wingate. He's on the rangy side, with a thick, butter-blond mane and deep-set slate-blue eyes. He moves with a lope that is at once awkward and graceful. He speaks deliberately, as if placing a special value on each word. And I must admit, I've always envied Jimmy's naturalness around things mechanical. His long bony fingers fit around a wrench the way a pianist's fingers fit against the ivories. My fingers drop things.

The Chevette started with a lurch. "Hmm," he said. "Guess I still don't have all the bugs out."

From the corner of my eye I could see Kevin and what's-his-name looking bored, lounging around the MacAllister lawn. They noticed us, and it seemed to bring them to life. Kevin poked the other kid on the arm, they exchanged a grin, then Kevin waved and ambled to our direction.

"Who's that?" Jimmy questioned, narrowing a glance at me. Only then did I realize my arm was moving up and down and I was smiling at the Great One out there, almost as if I actually knew him.

"You wouldn't believe me if I told you," I said.

The Chevette bounded forward as if reaching for escape. Leaving behind a cloud of exhaust and Kevin.

Safely away from Meridian Street and heading for the outskirts of town, Jimmy broke the silence. "So who was that guy?"

I told him. In detail.

He turned left at the Croghan Boulevard signal light and pointed the Chevette north, before giving in to a wide grin. "Oh sure. And I'm Clark Kent, otherwise known as Superman."

I shrugged. Didn't I figure he wouldn't buy it? But I was more certain than ever. The image of *that face*, inches away, just before Jimmy pulled his headlong flight, was still tantalizingly clear, hovering inside my mind like a bee hovering over pollen. The crisply curling maroon hair, those gorgeous green eyes fringed by black-black lashes, the elegantly chiseled nose—

"Besides," Jimmy cut in, his tone infuriatingly reasonable, "even if by some remote chance he was who you think he is, his name wouldn't be Kevin. He'd be an actor, playing a part, remember?"

I turned to eye him. This time I noticed that dumb pitted scar at the base of his cleft chin. The way his Adam's apple bobbed when he chewed bubble gum. The outsized knobs at his finger joints, which had been cracking since way back in the fifth grade. And the jogging shoes he wore like a second skin, grubby, tattered things with knotted laces, and the socks stretched out of shape and sagging to his ankles.

I looked away, somewhat less than enchanted.

"Tell you what," he said. "If he turns out to be that actor, I'll treat you to a steakburger special with milk shake at Hamburger Heaven." His lips curved upward in a smile that said, plainly, his money was safe. He consulted his watch. "Seven-thirty. Junior license only allows me on the road till nine. And tomorrow in the a.m. I'm due back at Uncle Steve's, bagging groceries."

FM radio music, accompanied by Jimmy's off-key humming and an occasional creaky howl from Camille, supplied the going-home conversation. I think Jimmy glanced over at me once, but since I'd closed my eyes, pretending to sleep, there is no way to prove it.

I could tell, way out there in the entry hall, that my father had already arrived. Mom and Danny had cornered him at one end of the sofa and were taking turns filling him in on the latest, while he took out his briar pipe and lit it. I stayed quiet, where I could listen, but not be seen.

Mom told him about the middle-aged couple and the two boys, who'd moved into the MacAllisters'. Of course she had to bring up the fact that I thought the tall, auburn-haired one was the TV soap actor who played Kevin Dowling. "Naturally I considered that preposterous," she added.

"Only, guess what, Dad," Danny piped up. "Suzy was right!"

Me, right? I could scarcely believe my ears.

It also developed that the other boy was the son of the show's producer, and the couple had been hired to chaperon them. "They'll be here for the summer," she said. "A combined vacation and development of the new story line—"

At which point, I made my presence known, with a "Hi!" Dad raised an arm in salute. Then everybody went back to talking.

Mrs. Wingate had found out that much and more. And she'd got it straight from the entertainment reporter of our newspaper, the *Fleet City Evening Star*.

Obviously underwhelmed by the whole bit, Dad yawned, then stretched his legs and aimed them toward a hassock. "A cup of coffee would certainly hit the spot right now," he murmured past his pipe stem. "I wonder if—"

"But, wait," Danny cut in. "The best is yet to come. When I was out at the Stokes place today, exploring, guess what I saw!"

Dad relit his briar, unleashed a ribbon of smoke and waited.

"Trucks, campers, movable scenery, cameras, a lot of guys running around, hollering orders—"

According to what Mrs. Wingate had heard, Hillsboro had been selected as a site for the *Days of Loving* on-location taping. "It's done often on the soaps," Mom said. "Until now, in exotic places like Paris, St. Croix, Barcelona..."

"Well, well," Dad muttered. I would say he actually seemed impressed. Still, with my father you never knew.

Naturally I'd do some crowing to whoever would listen. And some self-advertising. Humility is not one of my strengths.

Jimmy got the news from his mother and beat me to the phone. "Steakburger special tomorrow, after work," he promised grandly. "When I make a deal, I make a deal!" Followed by a throat-clearing pause.

He added, "Of course I won't get my paycheck till Friday. You'd better, uh, bring some money, just in case."

Behind me, Mom and Dad were speculating on why the Stokes place, of all possible sites, had been chosen. Mom considered it just another spooky old house with peeling paint and scarred-up gingerbread trim, on a lonely old gravel road too far from town to be useful. Dad had it pegged as common sense to go out of town. It would keep the crowds down and supply atmosphere, and there was plenty of room. Acres of it. "If I recall," he said, "old Leonard Stokes raised quite a bit of livestock out there. And that takes space."

"Barney used to get stuck with the livestock," Mom said. "Sometimes he'd come late to social studies, with his shoes muddied up and his eyes so red, you'd think he'd spent an hour behind the barn, crying."

"Barney Stokes, crying? I doubt that, Annie. The guy just wasn't a weeper type."

"Is that so? Barney had his vulnerable side, all right. I found that out, when I stumbled onto his little secret."

His eyesbrows shot up. "Meaning . . . ?"

"Meaning, if you'll wait until . . ." She nodded toward Danny and me. "We'll discuss it later."

Dad tapped his briar, took a puff and wheedled it back to life, then settled on the sofa as if planning to spend the next decade there. Mom grew suddenly very busy with a ski sweater she'd been knitting since the year one.

Danny and I got the message and escaped the pointed silence together. Beyond the house he went his way and I went mine, which was to call Molly and make a date for later in the evening.

Chapter Three

Molly came over bright and early the next morning. But I was a step ahead of her. Up before eight, dressed, ready to go.

My mother couldn't believe it. "On a Tuesday morning, in the summer? It's like a miracle! What's the catch, Suzy? And how much will it cost me?"

Molly and I had reasons unrelated to money.

As we headed out Molly said, "Mike Edwards called late last night. He wanted me to go swimming with him. Moonlight dipping, at the Buck Lake Cove." She paused on the second porch step. "Just the two of us. Mike and me. Know what that means?"

I looked knowledgeable.

"I'm not at all sure I'm ready for anything that involved," she said. "I mean, isn't summer for easy living, fun, meeting all sorts of guys and a little—what my mother calls, hanky-panky? I want to look over the field, keep it cool."

"Good thinking," I said.

"So I told Mike I needed the summer off. From him, and from the same old scene. I suggested he do the same. Date other girls. Hang out with a different crowd. Stir up the juices. And then in the fall we'll compare notes and see if we still have something going for us. He agreed."

"Smart move," I said.

By the time we'd negotiated the last step, I had our summer scene pretty neatly mapped out: Kevin for me, what's-his-name for Molly. Strangely enough, they were both standing outside the MacAllister house when we got there.

Were they expecting us? That possibility slowed me down, but not much; I was still inching forward, with Molly treading my heels and looking petrified.

"Over here, girls," Kevin said. He was smiling in a way that did interesting things to his tanned face.

"Courage," I muttered. From Molly, rattly breathing.

I bounced some clever opening remarks off my brain, then tucked them away for the exactly right moment. We'd made it to within a foot of the guys. I glanced up.

And straight into the eyes of Kevin Dowling.

Thinking back on it later, I relived the sensation of drowning in the turbulent green seas of those eyes, and reexamined, as through a hazy mirror, the perfectly shaped nose, the clean-cut line of jaw, the lips parting to form words.

What Kevin said was, "Hello there, beautiful." He said it to Molly.

Space in breathing. Then Molly said, *"Me?"*

He said, "Who else?"

I said nothing. Nothing at all.

Sombody coughed. The other guy, I think. There followed a rush of sound punctuated by bursts of laughter. We were into introductions.

"Kevin," it developed, was actually a person called Jack Faraday. The stunning blue Buick was his. "What's-his-name" became Sam, last name mumbled, leaving him semi-anonymous.

"I'm Suzanne Jensen," I heard myself contribute brightly. "Otherwise known as Suzy." My voice drifted off, as if sensing total lack of outside interest.

Molly and Kevin/Jack Faraday weren't saying much, unless prolonged eye contact tells it all. Blobs of pink stained her cheeks and a glow lit her face, as if she'd suddenly come down with a fever. I resisted the urge to break and run.

"He likes 'em skinny," Sam offered from behind his hand. "Takes all kinds, right?"

All kinds. Why did that make me feel as if I'd just been classified as part of a faceless mass of panting females herded just beyond the gate?

"My father's a producer on *Days of Loving*," Sam volunteered.

"So I heard," I muttered.

"Jack and I will be spending the summer here. At least, until the location scenes are taped. Pop figures since he'll be shuttling between Manhattan and Hillsboro, he'll stay at a hotel in the village. He says this will allow me to gain a sense of small-town living and a chance to experience independence. Then he hired this Mr. and Mrs. couple to stay here and keep a lid on us, just in case the independence goes to our heads." He paused and eyed me.

"Do you specialize in skinny girls, too?" I asked, grinning.

"Nothing fussy about me," he said. "I'll take 'em blond, brunette, redhead, noisy, shy, tall, short, chubby... not chubby..."

And where did I fit in? Suzy Jensen, not-so-skinny, with plain brown hair that frizzles when it's damp and hazel eyes that tilt above broad-boned cheeks. Not exactly your conventional beauty.

"Uh-oh," Sam muttered, glancing over his shoulder and losing the grin, "here they come. The groupies."

They came in pairs and threes and more, neighbors I'd known all my life, children of neighbors, Middle School kids who played with Danny and kids I hung out with in Hillsboro High, suddenly becoming noisy strangers, armed with paper and pen, all moving our way with one purpose in mind.

"Take my word for it. In a few days the thrill will wear off and Jack Faraday will be just another body on the block. But in the meantime... Hey, where are you going?"

Where? Home, where I belonged.

Beyond our living room picture window, females and a scattering of males of various ages were milling around, yakking, giggling, holding out pens. Autograph signing had become a brisk business on Meridian Street.

Sam had edged away, obviously trying to remove himself from the mob. But Molly was standing next to Jack, looking as if every inch of her belonged there.

"Back so soon?" my mother asked. "I'd have thought, given the excitement out there, you'd..."

"...be right in the middle?" I hauled my bones and flesh to the sofa and plunked them down. I sat there staring into space.

A small silence. Then, from Mom, "I'll be leaving shortly for the CPA's." My mother works a few hours a week for a local certified-public-accountant outfit. She often brings home enough paperwork to keep her busy on the evenings that Dad isn't here. "Suzy, if you find time to cut a row of Swiss chard, I'll freeze some later this afternoon. That shouldn't be too much to ask—"

"Mom," I cut in abruptly, "am I fat?"

"Of course not," she said.

My mother's figure has aged hardly at all. She'd been a baton twirler back when, and her 34-26-34 could still lead any parade in town.

"You take after the Jensens," she went on. "Their heavier bone structure and the slightly pigeon-toed way of walking. Even your father's Aunt Alice walks that way. And of course she has the Jensen bone structure."

My great-aunt hasn't seen her bone structure in years; it's not exactly a family secret that she lives mainly to eat.

"Oh, sure, she's put on weight. But she's such a good-natured soul. And a lot of fun at a party."

The last time Aunt Alice sat on our sofa, a cushion coil gave out. The groan and *boiing* of springs could be heard into the next room. She'd laughed louder than anyone. I wouldn't have, but then I guess I didn't inherit Aunt Alice's sense of humor.

I was definitely thinking "diet."

"As long as we're both here," Mom said, "why not join me for breakfast? Sausages, eggs, toast, orange juice—"

"Orange juice."

She frowned as I sipped at a glass of o.j. "That's your idea of a diet? Where's your protein and a spot of carbohydrate for balance? Listen, Suzy, if you insist on dieting, why don't we go at it the right way? With a checkup by the doctor and some common-sense menus—"

"*Mom!*"

"Although I still don't know why you want to lose weight. You look just fine to me."

She gathered up her dishes, rinsed and set them in the sink. Normally I do the same. But I kept on sitting there, staring at my empty o.j. glass and brooding. After a minute she wandered into the living room and to the picture window. "I do believe the crowd is thinning," she reported finally.

"Dandy," I muttered.

"What I don't understand," she said, "is why they came to Hillsboro, of all spots. And the Stokes place, at that. You'd think, when they have the pick of the world's exotic locations—"

Her voice rose and fell, pricking at the edge of my mind like a mosquito whirring just beyond a screen. But other thoughts were churning up and taking over.

I could see, again, Jack Faraday's sea-green eyes meet mine and then blink, as if whisking away something undesirable.

I'd never viewed myself as something undesirable. Not that every guy in town had been beating down my front door over the years, Jimmy Wingate had seen to that. Still, I'd had my moments, like, in the sixth grade, when Peter Raymond passed me that steamy little note, which our teacher, Miss Arnold, had intercepted, read to herself and snickered over before handing back. And during the eighth-grade picnic, Billy Andrews had kissed me.

We had been behind a giant oak tree, near Elijah Colman's barbwire fence, being spied on by a couple of his holstein heifers. It had been an interesting experience. At least that's what I told Jimmy later after he'd found Billy and me and an unfortunate fight had erupted, during which Jimmy's new striped shirt ripped and Billy received a beefy-looking left-eye job.

Actually I've mislabeled the experience as "interesting" because I don't know what else to call it. Billy Andrews kissed sloppily and kept his eyes closed the whole time. And he breathed funny. Ragged, sort of. I remember being immensely relieved when Jimmy finally showed.

And just last summer while Jimmy filled in his spare time on a farm, helping his Uncle Elton with the haying, and Molly was doing her usual stint in Chicago, I'd hung out with Marianne Freeman, whose older cousin, Joe, was visiting them for the month of July. The three of us were like buddies and went everywhere together. Then somehow it became just Joe and me, still buddies to the end.

Until one afternoon, while hiking through the woodlands, he'd broached a few startling suggestions about "love," and I said, "Forget it!" and he'd laughed and asked, "Are you kidding?" He'd chased me all through the brush. Then, like magic, up from nowhere loomed Jimmy Wingate. I can still remember the noise of male scrambling and Joe's rear view shrinking in the distance and Jimmy's face, streaked with sweat and dirt, and his eyes, lit with a kind of grim triumph.

The phone rang.

"Get that, Suzy, will you?" Mom called out.

It would have to be Molly. A person should be in a special mood, upbeat, good-natured, high on humanity, to tolerate a phone conversation with Molly Fancher when she's just tasted the fruits of unexpected success. I wasn't in the mood.

I listened with half an ear, catching tidbits about Jack's personality. "He has a sort of inner dignity, know what I mean?" she explained, and went on to tally his other fascinating features: the emerald green of those disturbing eyes, the length of his lashes, his sheer animal magnetism, whatever *that* was. "And when he invited me to go with him this afternoon to the Stokes place to watch the carpenters work on the sets, you could have floored me with a feather! I mean, *me*. Little old small-town me!"

My hearing came miraculously to life.

"Oh, by the way, I did bring your name up. I said, 'My best friend, Suzanne, will be absolutely devastated if she's not invited too.' And Jack said, 'Well, if she really wants to come.' And then I said—"

I snarled something decidedly uncouth.

"My, my, aren't we in a foul humor," she said. "And after I went to all that trouble—"

I let the receiver click into its cradle. With luck it would blast her eardrum.

My mother had picked up some information at the CPA office about the *Days of Loving* project. She came to tell me all the way out to the garden, where I was escaping it all, cutting Swiss chard with a heavy hand.

She started in with, "Suzy, you'll never guess what I just heard."

My fingers attacked a mess of greens, *clip-clipped* and dumped them into a paper sack. "You're right," I said. "I never will."

She had finally found out why Hillsboro was chosen, and why, especially, the Stokes place. The soap's producer was her ex-classmate, Barney Stokes, who, it developed, was quite a wheel in the TV series business. G. Bernard Stokes, executive producer in charge of momentous decisions, had apparently lowered himself to take charge of the grubby details of the on-location filming. And why? Because Hillsboro was his hometown and we were his people.

"The last time I saw Barney Stokes," Mom said, "he was definitely sour on Hillsboro, his father, his classmates, anything connected with the old hometown. He had a battered old suitcase and a train ticket to faraway places, and he was heading out and never coming back."

"Then that kid, Sam, is really Sam Stokes, son of..."

"Barney, and Lila Davies, lead actress of the long-running soap, *Search for My Love*. They divorced four years ago, a friendly split, no nasty resentments, no deep scars."

I had to admire Mom's talent for unearthing those details.

"It wasn't hard," she confessed. "Barney has a public relations person who goes on ahead, dropping bits here and there, all freshly sanitized, of course. What he and his personal life are actually like, we'll probably never know."

A little mystery to unravel. Was that what my summer needed?

Jimmy phoned at three, full of his own plans. "I'll pick you up in half an hour," he said. "Me and Camille, three-thirty sharp."

Something had to be better than nothing. Stupid me, I'd already shot down the only lively prospect of the day. Molly must be having a ball. After all, she had Jack Faraday hovering over her, hypnotizing with those eyes....

For a change I was ready when Jimmy got there. I'd vetoed the usual jeans and T-shirt, opting for this form-fitting sundress that, according to Mom, did things for me, I'd tamed the frizz from my hair, spraying it with something that smelled interesting and I'd put on the black shoes I save for special occasions. Why? I hadn't the foggiest.

"If I'd but known," Jimmy said, giving me the up-and-down eye, "I'd have sent the Cadillac and chauffeur." He'd strained himself to the extent of washing up and combing his hair and shrugging into something clean.

Camille, who didn't care what a person looked like, so long as he or she was human and close by, sat behind me with her tongue hanging out and flapping saliva with every breath. I could feel the wetness splat against my neck.

"Think nothing of it," Jimmy said comfortably. "Old dogs do that a lot."

He'd come into money; his Uncle Steve had coughed up advance pay. "Keep your nickels for a rainy day." He waved my offer aside and steered me into a back booth, allowing Camille to sneak past us, then hide under his feet. Every now and then the management got sticky about dogs bringing in fleas and germs and stuff; Jimmy figured there was no point in advertising.

"So what's your pleasure?" he asked, running a finger down the skimpy menu. "I promised you steakburger and milk shake, but if you'd rather have—"

"Tossed salad."

"Sa-lad? Rabbit food? Don't tell me you're on a *diet*."

"All right, I won't tell you."

"Why in the world would you want to lose weight?"

"When I'm so exquisite the way I am?"

"Well, yes, that could be said. I mean, I like the way you're put together, gently rounded here and there."

I thought of Jack Faraday's preference. "Some people think that today's woman should be slender, even bony, with narrow hips and the mere hint of a bosom. Some people—"

"Bull," Jimmy said.

"Like, for instance, take Molly Fancher. She—"

"You gotta be kidding. Molly has about as much shape as your kid brother."

"Well, she must have something. Kevin, I mean, Jack Faraday, snapped her up the way a fish snaps up bait. And I'm sure nobody twisted his arm."

"Jack Faraday must have sawdust between his ears if he fell for that skinny-minny. Far as I'm concerned, you're—"

Perfect. His eyes said it.

Gertie Adams, who's been waiting on tables since Noah floated the ark, hung in there, pencil poised. "Well, kids, what'll it be?"

"The steakburger special and a vanilla shake for me," Jimmy said. "And she'll have—"

"Hey, you guys!" Danny practically danced in and galloped to our booth. "Guess what?"

Sometimes, if I ignore him, my kid brother will go away. "Gertie," I said, "I'll have—"

"I've got a job." Danny took a breath, then let it all out at once. "I'm an official gofer. Which means I go for things. Using my ten-speed. Like, right now I'm supposed to pick up eight hamburgers and six colas and a dozen apple turnovers. Mr. Stokes, who's my new boss, says I can call him 'Barney'; he knows Mom and Dad from the old days. In fact, soon as he found out who I was, I was in. And I'll bet he'll hire you guys, too, 'cause they'll be doing that this week, hiring a few locals, I mean.

"Molly's already working on a job for herself. Got that Jack character pulling strings for her. I mentioned you as a possible, Suzy, and Jack said, 'Want me to put her name in, too?' And Molly said, 'I'll check with her to see if she can spare the time.' And I said, 'Are you kidding? My sister's got so much spare time, it's coming out of her ears.' And Molly said...'' Danny reached for another giant breath.

Gertie, who'd been shifting weight from one bunioned foot to the other and gazing ceiling-ward, jumped in with, "So what'll it be, Suzy?"

"Diet special," I shot back. "Tossed salad with the low-cal dressing. And diet root beer."

Chapter Four

Jimmy settled the job issue in his usual direct way. The next afternoon he drove out to the Stokes place and got jobs for both of us. "For me, part-time; that will fit in with stocking the shelves down at the Superette. Mine's not terribly exciting," he conceded. "Lugging lumber, hammering nails, throwing together rough sets and like that. On the other hand," he added, "yours sounds as though it has possibilities. Of course it may start with some heavy house-cleaning—"

"Oh, no!" That was Jimmy's idea of possibilities?

"But after that," he breezed on, "he's lined up these fun-type projects. For instance. Going through the junk in the Stokes family's attic and sorting out the goodies. Working with the prop man to set up the downstairs rooms for on-location scenes. And, who knows, maybe even a little acting. 'Extra' work, he calls it.''

" 'He' being the elusive Mr. Stokes?''

"Yeah. But always 'Barney,' not 'Mr. Stokes.' That's the way he likes it. And he's not being elusive, just very busy. And, hey, you want to hear something odd? When I mentioned your name, he said, 'Bob and Annie's daughter?' Naturally I said yes. He looked really pleased and he said, 'There. I've hired both her kids. Let's hope that helps to pay back . . .' Which was when his face turned red and he quit talking. Weird, huh?''

By then my brain had caught up with and was working on, "Maybe a little acting." And a shiver rattled through my bones. Acting? Me?

"The good word is, Molly will be working with you. I gather the macho kingpin, Faraday, did that for her. Boy, she sure is hung up on him. But I guess it's mutual. They hold hands and stare into each other's eyes and do a lot of eye-balling and whispering, that sort of soupy stuff.''

"Oh, great.'' Molly scarcely knew the boy. It certainly gave a person pause.

"The other kid, Barney's son, says Jack's okay, but he has some peculiar attitudes about women. Still, it could be sour grapes with Sam. As they say, some guys've got it and some guys don't. Right?''

It could also be said, so did some girls. . . .

Jimmy stuck around for supper. Mom always enjoyed his presence at our table. He'd eat *anything*, his speciality being leftovers.

Ordinarily, I'd join in with gusto. But that evening I somehow didn't feel like it, especially when I watched Jimmy reach for another slab of Mom's homemade raisin bread.

He caught my glance. "What's the matter, Suzy? Given up eating for the summer?" He slapped on some peanut butter. "Oh yeah, a diet."

I could swear I heard him snicker. But my scowling glance revealed only a bland facial expression made lumpy by a mouthful of raisin bread.

"By any rule of logic," Dad said, watching Jimmy's performance, "you should weigh at least three hundred pounds."

"My mother swears I have a tapeworm." Jimmy reached for his glass of milk. "She calls me the Wingate family garbage pail." And he washed down the whole mess with a swig of the white stuff.

Jimmy is his parents' "baby," the youngest of three. His married brother Paul lives in Baltimore, and his sister Elinor is a commercial artist upstate in Rochester. They manage to make it home often enough to give him a rough time. You could also state that, in the Wingate family circle, he's the barely tolerated kid brother, conveniently around to be teased or nagged or hollered at. I guess it says something for Jimmy that he never lets it get him down.

Speaking of kid brothers: during the dish-washing chores that followed our evening meal, Danny whizzed through his obligation by clearing the table in record time, then beating it out of there. Which left Mom washing and guess who drying.

One neat side effect of Jimmy's upbringing was his willingness to dry dishes. As I told Mom, guys *should* pitch in.

"Forget it, Suzy," she said, handing me a towel.

"But I dry them for my mother," Jimmy put in, still willing.

"And Suzy dries them for her mother," Mom said. Then she nudged me in the direction of the sink.

So much for equality of the sexes.

After a few seconds of weakening protest, Jimmy removed himself to our living room and in no time was absorbed in a TV rerun. Then Dad ambled into the kitchen, where he straddled a chair and fiddled with his pipe, cleared his throat and talked. While we were sudsing, rinsing, clanking porcelain and silverware, drying and stacking in the cupboard, this animated conversation wafted around me like a familiar breeze. Mom and Dad were exchanging news and views.

"Guess who I ran into downtown," Dad said between experimental puffs.

Mom swabbed out a coffee mug. "I've never been good at guessing games," she said.

"I was picking up my razor blades and a pouch of tobacco at the drugstore," Dad said, "when this tall, lanky guy walked over and said, 'Hello there, Bob

Jensen.' The voice sounded familiar. I took a good long look, and sure enough, it was Barney Stokes.''

"Barney?" Mom daubed at a spot on a plate. "Has he changed very much?"

"At quick glance, yes. The horn-rims are gone; he has contacts now. And the hair is graying at the temples and styled. Remember those butcherings old Leonard would do to the poor kid's locks? Those days are gone. Barney looks distinguished now. And self-assured.'' Dad let loose a thread of smoke. "Aah, yes," he said, "prosperity sticks out all over our Barney.''

"Really?" Mom rinsed the plate and popped it into the drainer. "I'm not amazed. I've always believed there was much more to Barney Stokes than Hillsboro would give him credit for.''

Beyond us, in the living room, Jimmy switched channels, tuned in to an action show that my mother hated and turned up the volume.

"Looking back," Dad said, "I place the blame squarely on the shoulders of Leonard Stokes. The way that man treated his only son was a crime.''

"It could have started earlier," Mom said. "The year his sister Louise got run down by the school bus. That must have taken the heart of his mother. I think the poor soul aged at least ten years that awful winter. And when the TB finally caught up with her—''

I dropped a fork.

Mom straightened abruptly and darted Dad one of her Significant Looks. He sighed, then laid down his briar pipe. "Suzy, why don't you and—" she nodded toward the living room "—your friend in there go outside and stir up some excitement? Your father will finish the drying."

Dad reluctantly took the towel. He closed the kitchen door with enough energy to almost sever my pinkie finger. I could hear the murmur of their voices rising and falling in conversation, as if they'd already forgotten me.

It took some doing to pry Jimmy loose from the shoot-'em-up-bang-bang! show. But during a commercial he gave in, and we wandered out to the porch.

Across the street, on the MacAllister lawn, Jack and Sam were setting up the badminton net. Molly, wearing a pair of white short-shorts that did interesting things for her legs, had arranged herself along the sidelines and was doling out how-to advice to which nobody seemed to be listening. The chaperons, Mr. and Mrs. Armbruster, imitating twin hunks of granite, had attached themselves to look-alike lawn chairs. Their combined scowls were keeping a gaggle of groupies at a respectable distance. Danny hung out there, too, just beyond the others, trying to appear as if he couldn't care less.

By the time Jimmy and I had overcome an initial siege of shyness, maneuvered past the security guard— tailgated by Danny—and made tracks across their lawn, Sam had cracked open some fresh shuttlecocks and was testing one for zip.

He seemed glad to see us. "I hope you guys go for badminton," he said. "I'm only temporary. Here till Pop shows." He glanced at his watch. "He's due at seven. It's already seven-thirty. That's my Pop," he said, working up a grin. "He'd be late to his own funeral."

Jimmy gave me the choice. "What say, Suzy? You want to, or you don't?"

My not-so-shy inner eye traveled the length of Jack Faraday, a thoroughly worthwhile trip, and focused in on the face. He was smiling in my direction. I interpreted the expression as friendly. As if he were actually noticing Suzy Jensen. And when the smile crept up to his eyes, I could definitely see me there. Something inside my chest gave a giant lurch. "We-e-ell, maybe."

I don't know why I allowed my gaze to stray just far enough to catch, full force, the storm clouds brewing inside Molly Fancher. It didn't require mind reading to get her message. "Uh, thanks anyway, but not tonight. Can we take a raincheck?"

"Ah, come on," Jack coaxed. "Put a little fun in your life!"

"Suzy always means what she says," Molly stuck in crisply. "So if we're going to start, let's—"

"Hey, I'll play," Danny piped up, eager as a puppy. "Say yes, Molly! Say yes."

"Yes, yes, yes," Molly practically shrieked. The storm clouds had fizzled away.

Jimmy and I returned to the front porch, sitting next to each other on a big old wicker sofa and dangling our feet over the top railing. We stayed there in cozy silence, our heads nodding to the beat of the shuttlecock as the streetlights winked to life.

Finally Jimmy broke the silence. "What time do you have?" Jimmy asked.

I checked my watch. "Nine o'clock."

He checked his. "Same as mine."

Across Meridian, Mr. and Mrs. Armbruster had shooed home the last groupie and were folding up their lawn chairs. The badminton game wound down quickly. Never-say-die Danny, still waving a mean racket, would have gone on forever, and the others seemed at least willing but Sam had mysteriously run out of steam.

While Jack took care of the net and Molly hunted down a mislaid shuttlecock, Sam moved over to the streetlight and consulted his timepiece. Then he surveyed the oncoming traffic, which consisted of one yellow Datsun heading north and a scarred-up red truck poking along south.

"Hey, Sam! What's keeping you?" From Jack.

"Coming," Sam said. But his voice sounded quavery, and in the glare of the overhead light his face looked blurred and tired.

Jimmy and I watched him pick a slow trail across the lawn, turning just once to make a final survey before disappearing past the MacAllister front door.

A pause, while Jimmy looked thoughtful. "Maybe Barney forgot to wind his watch," he finally came up with.

"Oh, sure! Tell me another."

"Hey, you haven't even met the man yet. Don't you think it's a little soon to form a judgment?"

Jimmy was right. Yet, I couldn't help wondering. Before this summer was over, how much more would any of us know about the real character of the "hometown boy," Barney Stokes?

I stayed on the front porch thinking about that long after the others had gone their separate ways. I only came to life when Dad hollered through his screened bedroom window, "Suzy, hit the sack."

Chapter Five

My mother has this thing about hanging out wet wash on nice summer mornings. The earlier, the better, especially on the days she's supposed to report to her CPA office duties. She ran three batches through the washer before seven-thirty that morning. Armed with full baskets and her precious bag of clothespins, which she lugged over to me for the hanging, of course.

"I do love the smell of clean laundry whipping dry in the warm breeze," she enthused, handing me a fistful of pins.

I creaked along a soggy flowered sheet and two pillowcases and muttered sour remarks under my breath.

My idea of fun does not include standing on our tiny back porch at eight a.m. reeling out sheets, socks, shirts and underwear.

From behind the nearby door Jimmy's voice sounded: "Hey, Suzy, you almost ready? We're due at Stokeses' by nine."

I glanced over my shoulder at Mom.

"It really isn't professional for her to show up late on her first working day," Jimmy pointed out. "And by my Timex it's—" his voice lowered to bass "—eight-thirty-one."

Bless that boy.

As I slammed the Chevette's passenger door and Jimmy reached toward the ignition key, Mom suddenly materialized. "Don't be surprised if Barney puts you to work washing windowpanes," she said. "That old house has lots and lots of grimy windows."

The rest of her words were swallowed up in the clatter-bang of the Chevette as it lurched forward.

"Windows," I grumbled to Jimmy as we sailed along. "Is that all my mother has on her mind?"

After what seemed miles of badly pitted macadam roads that led onto a narrow graveled lane that led onto what had to be a driveway, the Chevette chugged to a halt.

Jimmy hopped from the car. "Well, there she is," he announced, waving an arm, making a semicircle with his hand. "Your new nine-to-five place of business."

My eyes were drawn to the old house. I immediately thought of grayness. As if emptiness and nobody caring had drained it of all color.

"Yeah, I know," Jimmy said. "Kind of crummy, isn't it? But Barney insists that's exactly what the story line needs. 'An atmosphere of desolation,' he calls it."

Desolation. You could almost feel it sticking out from that beaten-down ark like fractured ribs.

Minutes later the action picked up considerably with the arrival of the crew. This turned out to be: a couple of sporty-looking bearded types lugging prop equipment; a not-so-young guy wearing a large brimmed hat and fancy Western boots, who I learned was Kirby Ashton, the assistant producer; and naturally, my kid brother poised on his ten-speed awaiting the slightest command from "the leader." I saw Molly and Jack in the distance, holding hands, of course, and recognized three boys from Hillsboro High, stars of the Bobcats football team, obviously there to supply muscle. Sam Stokes, looking glum, was hanging back from the others. A tall thin older man detached himself from the crowd and strode purposefully toward us.

"Hi there," he said, holding out a hand, "I'm Barney Stokes."

I liked his voice. Deep, pleasantly gravelly, not at all what I expected.

His eyes were brown and warm, and trained on me. "And you're, no, don't tell me, let me guess. Bob Jensen's child, for sure. I must say, if ever a girl looked like her old man, you do." He grabbed hold of my hand. "Bob and Annie's daughter. I couldn't be more pleased." And his fingers pressed mine in a firm grip.

I liked the way the corners of his eyes crinkled when he smiled. When his fingers finally let go, some of the warmth lingered.

At which point, Molly, never one to be outdone, had to ask, "Barney, would you say that I look more like my father or my mother?"

Barney zeroed in on her. Heavy space in time while he stared. "Your mother," he said at last. "In fact, you're the spitting image of Gladys, when..." His voice trickled away and hung there as if unsure of where to go. And then he said, briskly, "Well, kids, since we've come here to work, what say we get to it?"

It quickly became obvious that Barney Stokes possessed a gift for organizing. He'd assigned his noisy assistant, Kirby, to overseeing the "prop" team, the muscle boys to corralling two-by-fours and loosening slabs of siding from the rickety porch, Molly and me to cleaning out the third-floor attic and Jimmy, Jack and Sam to hammering together rough sets from the lumber.

There was one tense moment, when I glanced over at grim-visaged Sam, who must have heard the work orders but stood his ground, not budging. I watched Barney walk over and put his face next to his son's and speak softly, too softly for me to make out what he was saying. And then I saw Sam's face light up, as if the sun had finally risen after a very bad night.

The third-floor attic must have been the Stokes family's catchall. Its sixty-watt light bulb turned on to a perfect horror of cobwebs and dust mounds peering from dark corners, and elderly books spilling over wherever you gingerly stepped. At least somebody had left rat bait around to ward off furry little creatures. And Barney did mention that the hornets' nest under the window had been destroyed.

We cleaned off an area on the windowpane large enough to let in a glimmer of daylight. Through it we could see the set builders, sawing and hammering away.

Molly's eyes naturally focused on the busy body of Faraday. "You have to admit he's pretty special," she said.

I took a good long look and let loose an involuntary sigh. "You bet!"

"If you stare any harder," Molly said, "your eyes will pop."

It seemed safer to keep my gaze on Jimmy or Sam. Or, better yet, on the mess beneath our feet.

Cleaning up attic messes is not exactly Molly Fancher's cup of pekoe. She approached the whole ugly business with her usual reluctance. "I wouldn't be surprised if this touched off my asthma," she announced. Her fingers went to her throat. "Dust can do that, you know. Trigger an allergic reaction."

"As I recall," I countered, "you were desensitized to just about every type of dust particle going, the year we were ten. Remember?"

"Ah." She had another thought. "Still, wouldn't you think they'd want to keep the cobwebs, for background mood, for that important scene Jack tells me they plan on shooting up here?"

"Maybe they prefer to make their own cobwebs. More artistic or something." And then to catch up, I asked, "Important scene? Which important scene?"

"A fugitive is supposed to stash himself, or herself, in the attic, hiding from outside forces. But just who..."

"Probably Kevin Dowling. He could be classed as a fugitive. Or, hey, maybe Jessica Morgan. She did disappear first. I hope you're psychologically prepared for the femme who plays Jessica, since she's bound to show up here sooner or later. Have you caught her act on *Days of Loving* yet?"

Molly shook her head.

I laid it on. "The girl is absolutely gorgeous. And on the soap, she and Kevin seemed pret-ty cozy." Weighted pause. "Don't worry, Molly, but when it comes down to a competition between a local belle and Miss Beautiful of *Days of Loving* ..."

"Her name's Merilee Hayden; Jack's told me all about her, and I'm not worried one bit," Molly said, shrugging away that awful possibility. "They hate each other. Jack says she's a total nerd. Always wants her own way, upstages him every chance she gets, is generally obnoxious. And just before he left New York, they almost came to blows." Molly's smile said, *So there*.

It seemed only sensible to dig in and attack the attic rubble.

Wiping away cobwebs and sweeping and redepositing dust was no big deal. It was another story sorting out the Stokeses' family stuff.

"Barney did say, when in doubt, stack neatly in a far corner," Molly remembered.

We'd already set aside, for trashing, piles of twenty-year-old magazines and yellowing newspapers, when we came to those troublesome personal things.

Molly found it first, topping other keepsakes in an old overshoe box. A giant red construction-paper valentine bordered with white tissue lace. She read aloud the childishly formed words sprawled across it: "To Mommy and Daddy, I love you. Louise." She eyed me. "Who is this 'Louise'?"

"Barney's sister. She died when she was a kid." I enlarged on that. "She got run over by a school bus."

Molly's eyes narrowed. "Oh, sure."

"Would I lie to you?"

The corner of a picture frame stuck past the box rim. She made a grab for it.

A round-faced little girl with thick blondish braids stared up at us. The warm brown eyes you couldn't miss: Barney's, only larger, and spiked with dark lashes. And she had a gap-toothed pixie smile that would bewitch the town sourpuss into smiling back. The funny part was, she looked so alive. As if, with just a little magic, you could pluck her, whole, from the frame.

We stared at each other, then tumbled the rest of the stuff from the box.

There wasn't much. A few letters addressed to Mr. and Mrs. Leonard Stokes in Louise's crooked printing. She'd scrawled "S.W.A.K." on one envelope flap, and a peek inside revealed she was spending three weeks of that summer's vacation with her Aunt Josie in Syracuse and was having a "grate" time. A miniature doll with gaudy red hair, wearing a handmade powder-blue party dress, whose right arm was broken off at the elbow. A ring of fancy keys. One ice skate. Three nickels and a dime held together with masking tape. A fourth-grade report card showing mostly B-pluses. And a faded newspaper item recording the accidental death of Louise Mae Stokes, aged nine years, five months and two days.

We put the stuff back into the box. Carefully, this time, setting it in a far corner. And we returned to work with unaccustomed energy, neither of us volunteering a word until I spotted the yearbook.

"Hey, does that ever look familiar," I told Molly. "There's one just like it at our house, on an upstairs bookshelf. One of these days, when I'm hard up for something to do, maybe I'll fish the thing down and poke through it."

"Likewise," Molly said. "It has to belong to Barney. I mean, they did all graduate together, my parents, your parents and Barney."

"We've been knocking ourselves silly, bringing order out of this chaos," I said, putting my broom down. "I'd say we're ripe for some time off, to enjoy a few healthy laughs."

We turned to the *J* people first, zeroing in on Robert Jensen.

"There he is," Molly pointed out. "Star halfback, high-point senior on the school bowling team, member of the honor society. A real triple-threat man. Besides which, he was kind of cute back then. Not my type, true, but still..."

So much for Robert Jensen.

All right, on to Fancher. And there he was, on page twenty-nine, heading up the alphabetical *F* listing. Adam Fancher, with his soulful eyes, full lips, plenty of nose for his bony face and a scruff of curly hair that hung rakishly over a high-domed forehead. President of the Senior High Literary Club, vice-chairman of the debating team, three-year member of the drama group.

Molly traced a finger over the face of young Adam. "Hi, Daddy-O," she said softly. Did I detect a wicked gleam in the eyes that stared up at her?

"Enough of this," she said, suddenly tiring of the game. "Let's get back to work."

"Not on your life," I said. "For one, we still have the *S*'s." My mother, who'd been Ann Stafford, and Barney Stokes. "And your mother." Née Gladys Owens.

Barney Stokes. Who would believe it?

For one thing, that jig-jag excuse for a haircut, "butchering," Dad had labeled it, gave a strange, almost alien look to the gaunt, acne-marked face and the horn-rimmed glasses dominated his eyes, blurring their warmth, accenting a shyness that the Barney Stokes I'd met that day didn't seem to have.

"And did you notice," Molly pointed out, pursuing a fine point in our little game, "he has no extra-curricular activities listed?"

Sure enough, no varsity sports, no debating team, no honor society, not even a hint of membership in the drama group.

"I guess that's because his father kept his nose to the grindstone," I said. "From what Mom let drop I got the impression that Barney was just too busy with home chores to get in on the usual kid fun."

"I questioned my mother about him," Molly admitted. "She remembers Barney Stokes as a pleasant, quiet type who always kept up with his studies. He sat behind her in a couple of classes, and he'd let her copy his homework notes when she'd forgotten hers. She said she enjoyed teasing him because he would always rise to the bait and blush. Beyond that," Molly said, shrugging, "I guess he left no strong impression."

My mother the cheerleader came under scrutiny next. Her outdated hairdo had to be good for a loud howl from Molly. But I was reminded again, as I always am by early photos of Mom, how penny-bright pretty Annie Stafford had been back then. And I wished, as I so often did, that her genes had passed on that junior-size figure to me.

"Look." Molly shot out a forefinger. "She wrote something here under her picture. 'To Barney, who knows what friendship means.'" She looked up at me. "At least the poor guy had one friend."

He has his vulnerable side, Mom had said.

Molly flipped back a few pages. "And now...ta-daaa...! little Gladys Owens!" Followed by the comment, "Well, well, I do believe our Barney had found himself another friend. Because here's some more writing. 'To Barney, who was there when I needed him.'"

"The homework notes?"

"Probably. But... Oh, hi, Barney! I didn't hear you coming."

"I'm not really checking up." Barney smiled reassuringly. "Just wondered how business was progressing up here."

"Fine, until we hit your senior class yearbook," she said. "Naturally we couldn't resist a quick peek, to see how much you all have changed." She giggled. "Those pictures..."

"Oh?" The smile froze and died. Then he said, "You're to report, downstairs, to the noon lunch break, as of now. One half hour, kids, and that's it. On the double!"

We moved. On the double.

When we returned—exactly a half hour later—the shoe box had been shifted to safer quarters under the eaves.

The yearbook had vanished.

Chapter Six

Things did upgrade after a few days. Once we'd finished off the attic and licked and promised our way through the downstairs and recovered beer bottles from the front lawn, where couples from a nearby lovers' lane had tossed them, we could almost enjoy ourselves. Barney had laid down the law on the "extra" work. "What? Acting? You two? Forget it, kids." The highlights of each day had to be the lunch break and the 2:00 p.m. cola break.

Barney had arranged for all sorts of lunchtime goodies, but I stuck to mostly proteins and crisp salads, feeling pretty holy about my self-discipline.

"Exactly how much have you lost?" Molly had to inquire, one noon, while munching on a lemon meringue tart.

"That would be telling," I answered. I wished she'd picked better timing than a lull in the lunch table conversation.

"It does show a little around the cheekbone area," she conceded.

All three pounds must have disappeared from that area, because no other measurement seemed to have changed.

Jimmy had developed the habit of bringing Camille along with us. She proved to be a dandy waste disposal for dropped tidbits and under-the-table scraps. Jimmy soon perfected the fine art of knowing just where to drop them.

The three muscle boys, hereafter referred to as Jerry, Hank and Marshall, apparently got their kicks from recounting their romantic adventures with various girls they were dating.

Jimmy would always request that I leave the table when they got started. He'd suggest, behind his hand, that it would add nothing positive to my education to hear the sordid details.

I would stay. But after several sessions of who said what and who did or didn't do what to whom, during which they would look at each other and laugh, as if sharing some huge joke, I developed a kind of numbness in the head, an amnesia that blanked out sordid details.

As I'd said later to Molly, "After just so much of that sludge, what else is new, and who cares?"

"You're just not ready for adult discussion about perfectly natural human functions," Molly'd answered. And she and Jack had exchanged a glance that was supposed to show that they were.

All sorts of interesting characters would invade our lunch break. *Days of Loving* head writer, Mavis Lynn, a swift-walking, swift-talking redhead in her thirties, whose voice dominated the table patter, created the liveliest stir.

She and Barney fought running battles about such subjects as major story lines, long-range projections and fast-paced plots. She announced one afternoon that she watched *Days of Loving* every single day. "It's extremely important that the actors interpret their lines as I've conceived them," she said. She darted Jack a long searching look, as if trying to ferret out any objections.

Jack merely smiled and nodded. "Oh, you're so right, Mavis," he said. "You are so *right*."

She turned her glittery gaze onto the rest of us. "A head writer is like a musical composer," she said as we, her captive audience, hung on to every golden syllable. "We set the tone and the theme, and weave the subtle threads that make the story spring to life." She paused and glanced about, checking for attention.

I said, "Aha!" hoping that would help.

"We must know when to change a line that doesn't work. We must be able to ignore every unnecessary consideration and focus on just one: the shooting script, the script that gets on the air."

We had Mavis Lynn to thank for the small TVs, which she called monitors, that Barney placed in every room. She even placed a battery-operated one outside, under the giant sugar maple, where we sometimes sat during a break.

Meanwhile, back home on Meridian, dire things were happening. Two things. One more dire than the other.

First, the not-so-bad: Someone had sneaked into the MacAllister house while the Armbrusters were grocery shopping and lifted several of Jack's sportiest shirts, then planted cerise lipstick prints all over the wall next to his bed.

"Oh, not your gorgeous green flowered shirt," Molly wailed, overreacting, as usual. "I really loved that shirt!"

I mean, come *on*. It was only a shirt. Besides, his chocolate brown with the yellow polka dots, also lifted, was the real class act. That one deserved to be missed.

"And the lipstick on the wall," Molly burst out. "What were they trying to prove?"

"It's those dumb, stupid groupies." Jack scowled. "I hate groupies!"

"On the other hand," Sam volunteered cheerily, "what would you be without them? Just another pretty face on the cutting-room floor."

So, on to the biggie: Someone, it developed, had broken into the MacAllister garage and done a real job on Jack's Buick. They had flattened the whitewalls, spritzed the exterior with shaving cream that did shameful things to that glorious finish, scrawled obscene words along the back window with some black, tarry stuff that resisted disappearing.

"This is definitely not funny," Dad said, examining the damage. "I'd say, call the police."

Which was when Barney materialized on the scene.

It was all very friendly, with my mother supplying coffee and her special tea crisps, while Dad and Barney stood around, discussing.

Barney seemed less than eager to bring in the local law. "We prefer to keep a low profile on this type of incident," he said. "After all, we are on location, which means we're just guests here."

"Barney Stokes," Mom said, shaking a finger at him, "this is your hometown, and you'll never be considered 'just a guest' by the rest of us. You must know that."

He smiled almost too politely. I wasn't sure he believed what she'd just said.

The groupie problem came to an abrupt halt on Thursday afternoon, when classmates of Danny's, Laurie Allen and Kim Prather, were caught hiding under Jack's bed. Mrs. Armbruster happened onto them while dust mopping.

Laurie, whose body measurements suggested eighteen while her emotional level zeroed in at about six, raised a terrible fuss, screaming hysterically and kicking poor Mrs. Armbruster in a shin, settling down only after her father thundered in and made threatening gestures. Kim, a dumb-bunny follower of her chesty pal, came out from under, looking scared and blubbering.

The shirts were recovered, the cerise lipstick traced to its source. It came out, in the questioning that followed, that Ellis Peters, who had an unrequited thing for Laurie—who had a likewise thing for Jack—had vented his malice on the Buick. His parents would foot the repair bill, and Ellis would be grounded for the rest of the summer.

Jack felt much better about life after that. "These situations do crop up in our business," he said philosophically. "Which is why the chaperons. And why," he added, winging Molly a tender smile, "I have my little friend, here. To cool off the groupies and give me a stable image."

"And that's the plain, unvarnished truth," Sam muttered to nobody in particular. He caught my eye and looked quickly away.

Five of us, Jack, Molly, Sam, Jimmy and I, were seated around our kitchen table at the time, going over the day's excitement. They were guzzling milk shakes that my mother had set out there for them. I was working on diet cola, trying to ignore the milk shakes. Dad had left for Galveston that morning on another sales trip, and Mom had brought home piles of paperwork from the CPA office, keeping herself very busy at the dining room table and probably monitoring our conversation.

"I don't plan on staying in this end of the business forever," Jack was saying. "Acting is okay, when you're starting up the ladder. But the real where-it's-at is in directing. And producing. Control, that's what I'm after. Where I'm telling, not obeying." He slurped through his straw. "Obeying is for animals in the circus. 'Roll over,'" he mimicked. "'Balance that ball on your nose. Swing by your tail for the nice people.' Who needs it?"

"Isn't he *remarkable*?" Molly breathed, gazing up at Jack adoringly. Not at all her usual facial expression.

"Remarkable," Sam agreed. And he took two giant slurps.

"Sneer all you want," Jimmy said, "it still sounds like a hundred percent more fun than stocking shelves at the Superette. And I'll bet it pays better, too. Right?"

"One hundred percent. At least." Jack settled back in his chair and smiled.

My mother left her paperwork long enough to whip up another round of milk shakes. "From what I hear," she said, eyeing Jack, "drugs and alcohol have cut into the acting profession pretty badly. Have you, uh, noticed any such problem? I don't necessarily mean personally, but..."

"If you're asking, am I hooked on the stuff, the answer is absolutely not. I've no intention of muddying up my brain with mind-benders. The way I see it, if a guy's to get ahead in this business, he has to be sharp. And believe me, Mrs. Jensen, I intend to go ahead."

"Good for you," Mom said. She returned to her paperwork.

"You always manage to come through with your halo pure and shining," Sam aimed at Jack. "A rare talent."

"Thanks," Jack said, looking pretty pleased with himself. "I try. Sometimes I succeed."

After a few days on the job, I almost looked forward to rising early. I'd shower without complaint and put on fresh jeans, then wait, impatiently, for Jimmy to come by and pick me up.

During the first week Camille abandoned her back-of-the-head perch to scramble to the bucket seats, planting herself between Jimmy and me. She gradually worked herself onto my lap, from where she would sit up straight and stare out at the passing traffic.

Each morning, like clockwork, we rattled into the makeshift parking lot, where Jimmy stowed his Chevette far away from the other cars. He would park it behind a tree or some bushes, any place that would hide it from the eye. The other wheels, Barney's imposing Lincoln Continental, Jack's Buick, the clusters of exotic sports models and limousines belonging to the members of *Days of Loving* who rolled in and out of there daily, had given him a terrible complex.

This really bothered him. I mean, I'd never before known Jimmy Wingate to be embarrassed about owning something he'd worked so hard for and yearned over so much.

The second Monday morning I saw our esteemed leader watching, as Jimmy carefully buried the Chevette's traces behind a gnarled oak. Barney rubbed at his chin and looked thoughtful.

First thing, he set out chairs for all of us by the rusted water fountain gracing the back lawn and announced he'd assign chores for the week. Jerry, Hank and Marshall were to slap together the beginnings of a set to be erected in the kitchen, meant to make that room look even bleaker. "What we want to portray," he explained, "is a deserted, gloomy, decrepit old mansion."

"And you," he turned to Jimmy, "will be Fred White, the art director's, assistant." He let that sink in. "You will answer only to Fred. It's an exacting job, the man's a stickler for detail. He'll accept nothing but your best." Barney's smile was a tiny twist of the lower lip. "But you can handle it, Wingate. I have complete faith in you."

Jimmy's accepting smile was dazzling, opening up and lighting his face.

Was it just coincidence that during the lunch break Jimmy's Chevette showed up, as if by magic, in the parking lot, mere feet from a rose-toned Ferrari and an MG convertible?

Since the assistant producer, Kirby Ashton, had finally lost his voice, Jack and Sam were assigned to greeting the art director, two dialogue writers and whoever else wandered in, following them around and anticipating their every need, then doling out orders to Danny, everybody's boy Friday. This sounded like small potatoes to me. I mean, Jack was a *star*.

"I want to work this business from the ground up. Every facet," Jack said. "That's how you learn in this business, that's how you get ahead."

Molly beamed with pride. "Isn't he something?"

"He's something, all right," Sam said. I couldn't help noticing the irony in his tone.

I couldn't understand what was bugging Sam. He seemed so *grim* these days, especially when it came to anything connected with Jack. I'd figured them for such great pals.

Molly and I were assigned to the "prop" department. We were sent to dig through back closets for old hurricane lamps, frayed lace curtains, chipped cups and saucers, anything that would contribute to the shabby but genteel look of the "deserted mansion."

Molly spotted the dinnerware gathering dust in a small pantry. A handful of rose-patterned plates, cups and saucers webbed with a network of tiny cracks beneath their glaze. "Perfect," she crowed. "Just what we need!"

We nested a couple of cups and set them on the pantry floor, then reached in for saucers, turning around just in time to see Barney lumber along, arms loaded with paperwork. It was too late to holler a warning. His size twelves came crunching on the cups, full weight.

Barney dropped the paperwork. Sliding to his knees, he gathered up chunks of glazed rose. He hooked his pinkie finger into a cup handle and stared at it. "Ma's china," he said. He looked up at us. "I've destroyed Ma's good china."

Molly and I exchanged a stricken glance.

"She collected this pattern for years, trying to complete her set," he said. "One time, a dinner plate, the next, a cup...." He looked away. "Every Christmas I'd give her another piece. That last Christmas I got her a beauty. The gravy boat and ladle. But she never had a chance to—" He broke off. And when he glanced at us again, little windows had blinked shut behind his eyes. He bundled together the paperwork. "Get a dustpan and broom," he said gruffly. "Sweep the pieces up. Throw them out."

He turned on his heels and was gone.

Jimmy practically bubbled over, during the 2:00 p.m. cola break, reciting all the goodies about his new assignment and the virtues of Fred White; "no ogre after all, just a busy expert in his field who knew exactly what he wanted.

"We'll be working on the attic set soon," he confided. "Fred has this machine that manufactures cobwebs, and he's very fussy about arranging his cobwebs just so...." He stopped and glared at me. "What's so funny?"

It seemed safer to return to my diet cola. And after a loaded pause Jimmy returned to his monologue.

Finally he politely asked, "So how has the day gone for you?"

"Oh, average," I said, suddenly unwilling to discuss it. I'd already thought over the morning's happening. Who could miss the expression on Barney's face when he'd held the fragment of his mother's cup in his hand? It was as if that tiny piece of china had somehow tumbled him back to the past and rekindled an old hurt.

"Sam tells me that Barney's going back to the Big Apple for a couple of days," Jimmy said. "Something about pressures building up around here." He arched a brow. "I can't buy that, can you?"

I left his question hanging.

Life went on at the Stokes place, even without Barney. Kirby Ashton, miraculously cured of his laryngitis, filled in, creating frayed nerves with every tantrum. Still, we could survive anything—for two days.

Molly seemed more down than the rest of us. That didn't make sense. Didn't she have Jack Faraday?

It didn't help that so little in the way of amusement goes on in Hillsboro. Or that Jack was so paranoid about mob scenes. Let's face it, after you've been swimming at Buck Lake Cove, away from the frantic fans, and to the drive-in flicks, where darkness hides you from them all, and exploring the superexciting back roads, what was there?

"You can always trek into Fleet City," I reminded her. "Take in a class-act musical, the amusement park, the zoo—"

"Some help you are," she fumed. "You know Jack detests going where he'll be instantly recognized and drooled over by a pack of rock-headed females. And the *zoo*? Honestly, Suzy, sometimes you outdo yourself!"

"Do you get the feeling our hero is becoming a trifle restless? One might even say, bored?"

"Bored?" She looked shocked. Had I introduced a new, frightening thought? "A person with Jack Faraday's capacity for inner creativity does not become *bored*. And if you're referring to...well, what he and I have going for us..." She focused on the big toe of her sandaled left foot. "He's into 'career' right now; it's taking up most of his energies. He hasn't had time, lately, for—" her fingers brushed her lips "—romantic gestures." Pause. "But it really doesn't matter. I mean, we'll get back to that. For now I'm happy just to be around him and absorb all that magnetism."

Was she really? She certainly didn't look it.

Chapter Seven

I was standing around, taking in the soft summer
breeze, that Tuesday afternoon, when the feature
writer and staff photographer from *Daylight Soap
Drama Magazine* showed up. They'd got wind of the
on-location tapings. And since the *Days of Loving*
story line had become a hot item in the trade, stealing
more watchers from the other soaps each day, an interview with the stars was a "must."

Sharp-nosed Cora Wendell, whose every published
word was gobbled alive by soap fans the country over,
or so she assured us, seemed disappointed when she
heard that Merilee Hayden hadn't yet arrived.

"I wanted to profile you two as a couple," she told
Jack. "You do realize the world out there views you
that way?"

"A couple? Merilee and me?" Jack sounded horrified. "Yeah. Well. She won't be here for days." His facial expression added, *Thank heavens.*

From the corner of my eye I could see Molly stir from her nearby perch.

"So I'll save the profile for another day," Cora decided. "It is a shame, though." She brightened. "I could also use an item or two for my syndicated newspaper column, 'Afternoon TV Romances.'" Cora's column shows up in our daily, the *Fleet City Evening Star*, twice a week. "Nothing world-shaking, understand. Just a juicy bit about Jack Faraday that would tickle his many fans. If you have anything—"

Molly had moved with the speed of greased lightning. "Hi," she said, linking her arm with Jack's. "Somebody looking for me?"

Cora smiled. It wasn't a pretty sight. "Why, Jack, you young rascal," she said. "Holding out on the press, eh?"

"Oh, Molly's not my—"

"Molly?" She turned to Molly, who'd tightened her grip on Jack. "And what is your full name, dear?"

"Molly Owens Fancher," she pronounced distinctly, nodding her head and smiling, as if graciously acknowledging her public.

Cora had uncapped a pencil and was busily scribbling on a steno pad. "And how long have you and Jack been seeing each other?"

"Seeing each other?" Jack echoed. "Hey, wait, you're not going to print—"

"About three weeks," Molly cut in. "And I must say they've been the most wonderful weeks of my entire life." She glanced up through her lashes at Jack. He looked vaguely off into the middle distance.

By this time others on our crew, including Sam, had straggled over and were showing definite interest.

"Maybe we should get some pictures," Cora said, pointing her pencil at the photographer. "Just in case the Jack/Merilee profile falls flat. You never know, with these interviews."

Snap! Snap! Snap! Molly and Jack were preserved for posterity on black-and-white 35 mm film.

"You're a local girl, of course," Cora said, pencil hovering over pad.

"Of course," Molly agreed sunnily. "Which makes it all the more special. I mean, kids in Hillsboro hardly ever get the once-in-a-lifetime chance to meet and fall in love with—"

"Come *on*, Molly!" Jack had finally hauled his arm free and was glaring at her with a look that should have shriveled her.

Behind me Sam let out a sigh, as if he'd been holding his breath and could hold it no longer. "Okay, sport." He deepened his voice. "What say we tie up the small talk and get back to work? Barney will be back on Thursday, and you know how he gets when his schedule isn't followed."

The charged moment passed. Cora and friend disappeared down the gravel road, gunning their Chrysler, tooling on to the next "interview," I guess. We all hustled back to our chores.

Life around the Stokes place seemed tranquil enough, the rest of the afternoon. Unless, like me, you sensed certain undercurrents.

I'll confess I didn't just happen to be around, with ears tuned in, when Jack cornered Molly out beyond the back steps and they had that revealing little gab session. And I didn't just *happen* to be on the scene when Sam approached Jack immediately afterward and had *his* say. I was nearby, hidden by yewberry bushes and brush grass, taking it all in.

Molly had gone there to search for old bottles and other stuff for the "mansion" parlor and obviously wasn't prepared for a visitation from Jack, who practically loomed from the shadows to grab her by the arm.

"Ouch," she yelped. She looked up. Her yelp died away.

He let go of her arm. But his face stayed close to hers, and you didn't need ESP to spot the negative thoughts glowering there. "You shouldn't have done that," he said hoarsely. "You shouldn't have talked to that vulture!"

"Vulture? Oh, you mean Cora. She seems very nice. And so easy to talk to! Golly, Jack, I never thought I'd see the day I'd be not only interviewed, but photo—"

"Stop it!" Given that tone of voice, who wouldn't "stop it" instantly? "I didn't want you in the interview, can't you understand that? She'll make a big deal out of nothing, the way she always does; she'll twist it to say this and that; she'll make me look like some kind of..." He rooted around for the right word. Finding none, he went back to glowering.

"Are you telling me," Molly said, her voice rising, "that what we've had between us is nothing?"

"Well, not nothing," he amended. "But... Look, Molly, maybe we should reinterpret this. Let's put these three weeks into some sort of long view. You had a life before I came here, right?" Pause, while he waited in vain for her to nod agreement. "And you'll have a life after I go."

"But it won't be the same; it'll never be the same for me again! I can't tell you how really special—"

"Good. Because if there's one thing I cannot take right now, it's hearing how special I am."

Her mouth suddenly pursed, like a little kid about to bawl. I saw her rub at her eyes.

Jack looked faintly uncomfortable. "Okay, Molly," he said, "we'll postpone the heart-to-heart. Just hope, along with me, that Cora Wendell has more exciting things for her column than exaggerated stories about you and me."

He let her walk away, making no attempt to follow, not even when she turned and pinned him with a long wistful glance.

Conflicting emotions fought for dominance within me. On the one hand, I could feel, right down to my toes, Molly's confusion, her pain. On the other, there was Jack, of the hypnotic sea-green eyes, straining at her leash....

From beyond the steps, out by the tangled vines of an ancient strawberry patch, somebody coughed. And then I saw him. Sam Stokes. Moving speedily. Heading straight for Jack.

At first I could hear only low-pitched mutterings. Then Jack's voice strengthened to a scratchy growl. "All right, Sam, all *right*. I certainly wouldn't go out of my way to hurt the girl. But she's starting to get to me."

"She actually thinks she loves you," Sam said. "Can you beat it? And that poor kid's deluding herself that you could be in love with her, when we both know..."

"Aah, she's on some kind of ego trip. 'Local girl snags well-known soap star.' She may not realize she's doing it, Sam, but that girl is using me."

"*She's* using *you*?" A space, while Sam adjusted the squeak from his voice. "This is Jack Faraday speaking? You, the grand master of using?"

"Hey, just because you're Barney's son doesn't mean I have to stand here and take this!"

"Oh, that's right, you're a *star*. How could I forget?"

But Sam was shouting that to the rear view of Jack, who hadn't stuck around to listen.

Could it be that Sam was jealous?

Jealous. That had to be it.

On the following Wednesday just before supper my mother collected the *Evening Star* from the front hedges, where the paperperson had tossed it while aiming for our porch. She leafed through it, catching Cora Wendell's column almost immediately. "Oh my goodness," she said, "can you believe this?" And without waiting for a reply from me, she read aloud, " 'That popular young star of *Days of Loving*, Jack Faraday, is making the most of his on-location stay in upstate Hillsboro. Jack and a delectable local honey, Molly Fancher, are closerthanthis.' " She looked up. "How in the world did Cora Wendell get wind of that?"

The phone rang. Just in time.

It was Mrs. Fancher, and there were long stretches in the conversation in which my mother did nothing but listen. As soon as she got off the line, I pumped her for information.

What Mrs. Fancher said boiled down to she was on cloud nine about the item, she considered Jack the greatest. He was clean-cut, polite, didn't drink, didn't smoke, didn't do drugs. And, no, Molly hadn't yet seen the item, but she did receive an urgent phone call from Jack, who said he'd pick her up with the Buick in two minutes flat and Molly had grabbed up her jacket and beat it. What apparently puzzled Mrs. Fancher was why Molly had appeared upset by his call.

I had no answers to that one. At least, none that I cared to mention out loud.

Jimmy came over later and, breaking open a new deck of cards, looked hopeful. "Gin rummy, anyone?"

I volunteered. I had my reasons.

Molly phoned around ten, cutting in on a game we'd been nursing along for what seemed hours. "Suzy?"

Her voice came through raspy. The asthma?

"A touch of laryngitis," she explained it away. "Listen, what I'm calling about—"

"Hey," Jimmy interjected, "do we have a game here, or don't we? Of course if you prefer to concede defeat..."

"I'll be going away for a while. To visit Daddy and...and that woman. Maybe for a week, maybe for the rest of the summer, who knows?"

"Care to say why?"

She coughed, and this jagged, bubbly sound erupted. "Because I'm sick of this town, that's why! I tell you, I am fed up to my eyeteeth with everything—everybody—"

"Molly? Are you crying?"

"C-crying? Of course not!"

"Okay, okay, now let's think this through. You're going to blow out of Hillsboro like a storm cloud on the run and expect no questions? For instance, Jack will wonder..."

"After what he said to me, who cares?" she declared, hitting a high note.

"But most people think that you and Jack—"

"Most people can think what they want! If you must know, I'm getting pretty tired of Jack and his childish behavior. And, Suzy, if you'll recall, I did plan on playing the field. New faces, new experiences..."

"I thought your father had other ideas. I mean, what with the new bride and all those marital adjustments—"

"I'm still his daughter," Molly said. "The only one he's got."

"Well," I said, "if your mind's made up—"

"It is."

I struggled for something upbeat to say but only came out with, "See ya, Molly. Take care."

I rehooked the phone receiver, then stared at it, trying to unscramble my emotions.

"Something bothering our Molly?" Jimmy inquired, gathering up the rummy cards.

"Yeah."

Jimmy set the cards out, methodically building up each suit from ace to king. "Things are kaput between her and Faraday?"

I nodded.

"His fault?"

I didn't know what to answer.

"Aah, probably hers. You know what a hardhead Molly can be."

It could be so stated. Maybe things would have been different if she hadn't been so possessive about him or hadn't assumed it was the 'big thing' for Jack that it seemed to be for her.

Jimmy topped the ten of hearts with a jack. "You could say Molly's like a tasty McIntosh apple that's dotted with blemishes. If you're high on MacIntosh apples—you'll accept what you've got, blemishes and all." He slapped a queen onto the jack. "That's my last official word on Molly Fancher. How about a little birch beer, to soothe the savage throat?"

I passed the full-length mirror in the entry hall, on my trip to the kitchen for Jimmy's birch beer. The mirror was still there when I came out. I slowed to a stop before it and eyed myself.

I ruffled my hair. Hmm. Maybe a new cut. And some decent makeup that would highlight the hollows in my cheeks. I took measure of the rest of me. Hey, the hips actually looked smaller. And my waistline...

"Birch beer," Jimmy called out. "Remember?"

I hurried from the entry hall and back to Jimmy.

The subject of Molly and her troubles dominated the conversation on Jimmy's and my trip into work the next morning.

Jimmy was inclined to be philosophical. "What will be will be," he said. "Either way, Molly'll survive. Besides, Chicago's full of eligible guys. Molly's not blind. She'll notice."

Such easy answers. I wished I felt as secure about Molly's reactions as Jimmy apparently did. But then,

Jimmy wasn't nursing a sense of guilt. Still, why should I feel funny about wanting to develop something with Jack, now that Molly was out of his picture? Who would I be hurting?

I did consider exploring this angle with Jimmy. But why muddy up the neat little world we'd created for ourselves over the years?

Barney had arrived ahead of us. And he'd noticed immediately that Molly wasn't around. "Say, do any of you know why she isn't here?"

Thick silence, while his eyes traveled from face to face and came to rest on Jack's. "Well? Surely you can tell me, Faraday."

"Oh, you know how girls are." Jack shrugged, not quite meeting Barney's gaze. "Sometimes they get overemotional about the dumbest things."

"Oh?" Barney's eyebrows headed for his hairline.

"She did say something about visiting her father in Chicago," I finally offered. "At least that's what my mother told me Mrs. Fancher told her—"

"Your mother? Ah, good, then Annie can give me the *real* lowdown. I'll call her."

He used the extension phone beyond the rehearsal hall to call Mom. From where I stood, just outside the door, his end of the conversation came through loud and clear.

"Annie? Barney, here. I understand Molly's headed for Chicago. Could you enlighten me as to why?" Lengthy pause, during which Barney said nothing at all. Then he said, "I don't doubt it one bit, Annie.

We've had problems with artistic temperament before. It's always a headache, but temperament goes with the territory. Right now I'd like to wring his young neck. We certainly do owe Gladys an explanation. Or an apology, depending on the heat the kid generated. I'd appreciate it mightily, Annie, if you'd convey to her my... What? Me? Oh, I don't know, maybe we'd better forget the whole... Chicken? Who's chicken?" I could hear him breathing. And then he said, "Okay, I'll phone her. Later. Tonight, if I can, or maybe sometime tomorrow. All right with you?"

Barney clanged the receiver in its hook and turned abruptly, forcing me to move away from the door with unaccustomed speed. I tried to appear nonchalant as he hurried right on past me.

A few minutes later he strolled over. "Oh, by the way, Suzy," he said, "next time, don't stand outside the door listening. Come on in, where you can catch every word."

The next day Betsy Egan, Molly's replacement, arrived on the scene. Betsy is totally likeable. Hardworking, considerate, easygoing, with a bubbly sense of humor. All the things Molly's never been. And yet... she wasn't Molly.

Somebody else was missing Molly, too. Sam Stokes came over to me that Thursday morning and, after a mouthful of small talk, asked, "How long did she say she'll be gone?"

"Maybe for a week, maybe for the rest of the summer."

"The rest of the summer?" He caught my eye. Then he shrugged, as if it didn't really matter, but I'd caught the stricken expression on his face.

He and Jack were still speaking at that point, but if some shreds of friendship remained, they'd been placed on hold. Sam stuck pretty close to his father's heels, hanging out with Barney after hours, staying as far away from Jack as possible. And Jack had suddenly developed this overwhelming desire to work, pouring himself into all facets of his craft as if his life depended on it.

"At least he's ambitious," I pointed out to my mother. "That's what you're always trying to drum into me. Be ambitious, keep your nose to the grindstone, pursue your goals."

"I did say that," Mom conceded. "Wonder if I should eat my words."

Otherwise, events at the Stokes place hummed along. Story conferences cropped up as a few more scripts began to arrive—accompanied by Mavis and a couple of dialogue writers. A skeleton camera crew flew in one day, conferred and flew back to NYC. We'd moved on to total involvement, erecting the sets, working toward the final polishing before the rest of the cast showed.

And then it happened. The arrival of Merilee Hayden.

Jimmy and I were on our cola break, standing around exchanging chatter, when the long amber dreamboat crunched against the driveway gravel. And we watched, together, as Merilee/Jessica flipped off the ignition and eased an elbow onto the rolled-down window. "Hi there," she said.

Hi there. Two dinky little words uttered matter-of-factly by a girl in a Porsche.

Even though I'd viewed "Jessical Morgan" X number of times on the twenty-five inch screen, I wasn't prepared for Merilee Hayden.

She opened the car door and slid out. Naturally, I gave her the once over, jealously noting her shining shoulder-length hair, her flawless skin, and her huge eyes the color of ripe blackberries. When she smiled, she exposed her neat little even teeth. Need I add that her figure was stunning?

Most of the work crew were elsewhere doing their thing, but Jack Faraday was definitely around. He'd propped himself against a nearby tree trunk and was filing his fingernails, looking fully absorbed in his task.

Somebody had to speak. "Hi, Merilee," I greeted brightly. "We've been sort of expecting you." I turned to Jimmy. "Maybe you could collect her luggage?" Pause. I said, "Jimmy?"

The body was still there, but the rest of Jimmy had gone comatose, as surely as if he'd been slugged on the head with a sledgehammer.

Merilee's glance swept the terrain, freezing slightly when it caught up to Jack. She extended a small hand to Jimmy. "Your name is...?"

"I'm James. Yeah. James T. Wingate."

Her fingers pressed against his right wrist as if checking for a pulse. "Aah, Jamie. As you may have gathered, I'm Merilee Hayden."

The sound of nail filing picked up briskly.

Jimmy's lips moved. "Mer-i-lee?" A lamp suddenly snapped on behind his eyes, lighting up his whole face.

Her fingers lingered there, pulling away only when Barney hollered from somewhere beyond us, "Hey, Merilee! Shake a leg!"

I watched Jimmy watching her. And then all at once I couldn't watch any more.

A kind of emptiness had invaded my stomach, leaving a big cavity where my last cola had been.

Camille, who'd been preserving her energy by lounging in the shade cast by Jimmy's Chevette, suddenly became all wagging tail, jumping up and down, putting in a bid for attention.

"I guess she wants to be introduced," Jimmy said. He corralled his little pal and held her out. "Merilee Hayden, meet my friend Camille."

Merilee extended dainty fingers and touched the roughened fur. "Ah, so. Camille. Very nice." Her lips parted, all of those perfectly formed ivories showing in an irresistible smile.

Wriggling free of Jimmy, Camille headed for a large rock, behind which she at on her haunches and snapped at flies.

Jack pocketed the nail file and removed his spine from the tree. "Well, here she is. Merilee Hayden, girl of the hour." He ambled our way and caught my eye. Had he finally recognized me? Me, Suzy, a girl?

"Suzanne Jensen!" He reached out and grabbed my hands. "Where have you been keeping your sweet self?"

"Why, uh, here, where I've been all along?" A pulse beat tom-tommed like crazy at my throat. I considered pulling away my hands. Then I reconsidered.

"Merilee!" Barney's tone had sharpened.

Only after Merilee had collared Jimmy and they'd moved along, did Jack go about his chores. The glance he'd leveled at me lingered like a tantalizing whiff of incense.

Chapter Eight

I think I floated through that afternoon. And when Jack stopped by to say he'd love to drive me home after work, I barely stammered yes. Then I hightailed it over to Jimmy with my news.

I found him with Merilee. She was seated next to him in the Chevette, and he was listening intently to her, as if appreciating heavenly music. He jumped when I tapped him on the shoulder.

"What? You're actually going to ride in that sleek businessman's special with the Great Faraday?" Merilee had to put in her two cents. "He really thinks he's Mr. Cool. Faraday, the rising young executive, temporarily sidetracked by stardom." She laughed this tinkly little sound. "Well, let me tell you, I'd rather ride, any day, in Jamie's nice little..." Dangled pause, while she word searched. "Chevette," she came through triumphantly. "I like my men *real*. And unpretentious. Men who drive cars as unpretentious as they are."

This, from the girl in the gold-flecked Porsche.

Jimmy looked dazed, as if the anesthetic hadn't yet worn off. "Fine, Suzy," he said, smiling dewily. "We'll talk later."

Sure we will, I thought, and was surprised by my own bitterness.

Hey, wasn't this what I wanted? Jack, actually interested in me? And only good things for my old pal, Jimmy?

It was a heady experience, sitting next to Jack Faraday, as we zoomed down Hillsboro's roads in that long, beautiful hunk of auto. And I couldn't help but wonder how Merilee would enjoy clunking along in the Chevette, with Camille slapping saliva against the back of her neck. Now, there was an experience not to be missed!

On the way home Jack mentioned movies. I said, "Where?" He said drive-in. I said, "Fine with me," while the tom-tom beat like mad at my throat. A real live date with Jack!

My mother, however, did not share my feeling of elation when I told her about it.

"After the way he dropped Molly? Suzy, what are you thinking?"

"I'm thinking that Molly's worst enemy is still Molly," I said. "She always did overreact. We both know that."

"But do you trust him? You must admit the boy's been around, more than any boy here in Hillsboro has. Are you sure you can handle..."

"I can handle it."

"I wish your father were here," she said. "I could use his support."

I wandered back to the hall mirror and did a slow scan. It had to be the lost poundage, I decided. Because, otherwise, the person staring back was the same old me. Still, Jack had asked me out. There had to be some reason.

The preliminaries went well enough. I'd searched the length and breadth of my closet and had come up with my blue slip-on shoes and black lace panty hose and the blue polyester number with the three-tiered off-the-shoulder ruffles that Mom had spotted in the Sears catalog—I'd spurned it as too, too much but she'd bought it anyway. We left the house without the expected noise from my mother or the usual wise remarks from Danny.

When we got to the drive-in, Jack planted his Buick close enough to the screen to allow us to live along with the characters on the screen. It was a good thing I'd already seen the movie—in May, at the Bijou—because during the first half, Jack launched into a running monologue of what was about to happen, scene by scene, and full details of how the experts had created those special effects. I tried to appreciate the fact that Jack was hung up on special effects and endless other film stuff, but I found my attention wandering as he rambled. I focused on other area cars, wondering who the couples behind the many steering wheels were and hoping they could see and recognize the guy nestled beside me.

"Look, Jack," I cut in, tugging at his sleeve and pointing. "Friends." Namely, Jimmy and Merilee, buddy-close, in the plush seats of her Porsche.

"Aha," Jack said, sitting up straight and glaring past his open window, "you might guess she'd bring the Porsche! After all that chatter about riding in a humble little car with a good old hometown boy."

I thought of telling him the probable reason for the Porsche: Jimmy's junior license wouldn't permit him to drive past 9:00 p.m.

Jack's glare settled on Jimmy. "Good night, he's only a kid. What's she trying to prove?"

I slid down in my seat and said nothing.

Jimmy spied us. He waved and smiled. "Hi, you all! Classy bus, here, right?"

Half a dozen windows rolled down, and suddenly there was an audience. "Hey, it's a Porsche!" and, "Wow! Ain't that something!" and, "Get that gold fleck, will ya!" A woman noticed Merilee and said loudly, "Frank, it's that girl. You know. The one on the soap opera. Jessica! Jessica Morgan!"

There was a minor stampede to the car, and all sorts of objects were hauled out to be autographed. Then, after a decent interval, Merilee smiled, murmured something gracious and waggled her fingers, and the crowd obediently melted back to their upholstered interiors.

"She just loves all that attention," Jack stewed, beside me. "I cannot understand that girl. She eats it up!"

The screen came to life with the second half of the movie. Inside the Buick we watched the special effects with almost no comment from Jack. He had become strangely preoccupied, and in the middle of a really hairy chase scene, his glance strayed to the Porsche.

Things seemed pretty cozy over there. It must have been catching, because the next thing I knew, Jack's arm had crept around my shoulder and we watched the rest of the show more or less head to head.

After the movie we stopped at Hamburger Heaven. Jack aimed for the farthest booth and whipped out a pair of wire-rim glasses that made him look like a hundred other guys with glasses. And when Gertie Adams plodded over to take our order, he kept his voice down to a mumble.

"Seems funny not to see you with young Jimmy, over there." She nodded in the direction of a well-lit front booth, where Jimmy and Merilee were holding court. "You two kids been like a together item since you were small. And it sure does seem odd . . .

No offense," she added kindly to Jack.

He glowered. "Cubed steak with baked spud and peas."

"I sure did hate to see little Molly take off for Chicago! It did the girl good to spend the summer here in Hillsboro for a change, instead of traipsing off to God knows what in the big lonely city. I—"

"What'll you have, Suzy?" Jack cut it short.

I surprised myself by ordering steakburger with all the trimmings and a large slab of pecan pie. What was I doing to myself? I mean, after all those weeks of semistarvation!

Jerry, Hank and Marshall were whooping up a storm at the booth across from Jimmy's, trying to catch Merilee's eye and ear. But she simply overlooked them, the way you overlook a child who is screaming for attention.

Jimmy received the tab from Gertie, studied it, then helped Merilee to her feet. "Gotta get the girl back to the Lambert Hotel," he announced to whoever might be listening. "Big day on the set tomorrow."

"Oh, sure," Jack muttered. "She drops him off home like he's her little brother, then she drives herself to the hotel. Some romance."

Loud, raunchy noises from the three musclemen. Not a glance from Merilee. Jimmy paid, then held the door for her. Together they moved out into the starry night. I bit into my pecan pie, gobbling it down as if I hadn't eaten in twenty years.

Jack craned his neck. "Did you see the wad of change that kid left the waitress?" he croaked, gesturing toward the front booth. "Who does he think he is? The town millionaire?"

The evening ended on this slightly sour note. When Jack delivered me to our front door, he barely brushed my lips with a good-night kiss. It briefly occurred to me that I'd received livelier action from Billy Andrews, back when, at the eighth-grade picnic.

Jimmy picked me up the next morning at the usual time. He was in a great humor.

Of course his conversation immediately veered to Merilee. "She says I remind her of a character in a Norman Rockwell illustration. She says she's very high on Rockwell right now." He turned to me, grinning. "And you won't hear me knocking that.... By the way, I was sort of surprised to see you and Faraday at the drive-in. You have a good time?"

"Not to change the subject," I said, "but haven't you forgotten someone? Like your little buddy, Camille?"

"Oh. Yeah. Camille." The smile faded, then worked itself carefully back. "I decided to leave her home. As Merilee says, it's really no place for a dog. She'll only get sick on the scraps of food that everyone's been feeding her. And Merilee figures, what with all the cars coming in and out and Camille not moving as fast as she used to, she could get hit. And we wouldn't want that. As Merilee says..."

It would appear that Merilee had a lot to say. I laced my fingers across my knees and stared past the window. When we stopped for the light at the intersection of Main and Parkhurst Avenue, where Camille usually abandoned the space between Jimmy and me to edge onto my lap, I kept my mouth shut and my gaze fixed on the traffic.

Business had picked up in the Stokes parking lot. We were being invaded by people from the lighting department, the head guru of the camera crew, the actor who portrayed Josh Morgan—Jessica's police detective brother—and, finally, the man who would direct the story line. Things were building toward *real* action. Rehearsals were about to start. We locals would soon be phased out.

The publicity department of *Days of Loving* had set up an interview with the entertainment reporter of the *Fleet City Evening Star*.

The soap's on-location director, Gerard McVane, was chosen to handle it. McVane was a short, round-faced man with a shiny head showing through carefully arranged strands of beige-toned hair. During the interview he held his own.

For instance, when the reporter asked, "What, in your opinion, makes *Days of Loving* stand out from the other daytime dramas?" he had an immediate answer: "Our cast and story lines have gone younger. We've quickened the plot pace. We leave the preaching to the preachers, the messages to the U.S. Postal Service. We entertain, pure and simple. A little melodrama, a lot of suspense, a couple of romances heating up—one boiling on the front burner, the other simmering on the back burner. In fact," he added, smiling, "we're now building a young romance between..." McVane's neck swiveled, his gaze settling on Jack.

Jack eyed him coldly and looked away.

McVane's glance slithered to Merilee, searching for encouragement.

Merilee's lips came together and furrowed like a prune. She stared stonily back.

McVane shifted his sights back to the reporter. "Well, uh," he said, "let's just call it...back burner, heating slowly."

"Hey," Danny stage-whispered from behind his hand to Jimmy, "do you get the feeling all is not honey-sweet with our back-burner couple?" Danny had developed an awe-filled crush on Merilee, complete with pedestal and statue. "I mean, between Jack and Merilee, definitely bad vibes. Right?"

"Ri-i-ght." Jimmy appeared totally at home with that knowledge.

The interview did provide some pluses. The reporter had noticed their unexpected coldness and had mentioned it in the *Evening Star*, speculating as to why, building up the incident's importance, which should have helped the ratings, and brought Jack Faraday back into my picture for several nights running.

Jack preferred pretzels to chips, liked his ginger ale chilled, and his ice cream, pistachio mint, with a sprinkle of nuts. He watched certain television shows with an eagle eye, spotting the slightest blooper or unthreading of plot line. It was stimulating, just seeing him in action.

"Action," my mother echoed, when I brought this to her attention. "The only action around here is one of us scooting about for another bag of pretzels or presenting his lordship with a chilled glass of ginger ale."

"But—"

"And another thing," she steamrolled on. "Your father is due back from Galveston tomorrow. And I'm sure he won't relish Jack switching channels in the middle of one of his precious New York Mets games."

The working crews were dwindling. Kirby Ashton had gone back to the studio to supervise. The locals, Jerry, Hank and Marshall, had been laid off the day before. Betsy, thinking ahead, just up and quit. Danny had become a fixture, Barney's personal gofer; he would have had to throw the kid out bodily to get him to leave. I figured on sticking around for a while, trying to appear useful while I watched.

Jimmy and Sam would shortly be assisting the lighting director, which must have pleased Jimmy, who was developing quite a knack with technical equipment.

One day after a rehearsal Jimmy and I were given the afternoon off.

We drove out into pure country, past his Uncle Elton's farmland, past the You Are Now Leaving Hillsboro sign, to a brambly graveled road we'd often bike-hiked to. We found, again, that stretch of tangled brush, where the raspberries could be had for the picking, and one person could talk quietly while the other listened.

I listened, Jimmy talked. About Merilee. Her beauty, her lively personality, the thread of common sense that ran through her like a strand of cotton through silk. "And to think, with all the glamor guys she's known, and who must be crazy about her, she prefers me." He shook his head, as if still reeling from that shock.

"Well, why shouldn't she?"

"Her Aunt Shelley keeps calling me a rare specimen. She says they don't make guys like me anymore. She always sort of snickers after she says that." Jimmy frowned at his knuckles. "I don't think her Aunt Shelley likes me very much."

"That's impossible! Everybody likes you."

"Well, it doesn't really matter. I guess nothing matters except what Merilee thinks." He leaned back in his seat and looked blissful. "And I know what she thinks."

It was not the moment to bring up any reservations I might have about Merilee Hayden's character. "She is a little older than you," I pointed out.

"Thirteen months older," he conceded. The slate-blue eyes became dreamy. "Still, in life's grand scheme, what's thirteen months?"

"A year and thirty days," I said.

But it didn't register. "Oh, I realize there'll be other guys along the way with more experience, more sophistication, waiting like a bunch of jackals." He focused. "Hey, I have a thought! Maybe I could grow...you know." His forefinger grazed his upper lip. "Foliage."

"You have to be kidding!"

"It would be, like a symbol. Of the *real* James T. Wingate. Know what I mean?"

I chose my words carefully. "To begin with, blond guys usually have trouble sprouting, uh, foliage overnight. You may be all summer cultivating."

"So? I'll be here all summer. And who knows? By fall..." His forefinger strayed from the upper lip to the cleft in his chin. "More foliage."

His smile broke through like a sliver of bright sun.

Chapter Nine

The aroma of simmering pipe tobacco rippled forth to greet me as I trotted to our front door. My father's pungent mixture of apple and black cherry.

Do delicious aromas linger like old memories in the mind, wafting back years later, whenever we need them? If they do, I know that wherever I roam in life, that particular fragrance will zero in an image of my dad, home from another trip, slumped on the sofa, eyes closed, a ribbon of smoke lazily wreathing his balding head.

His eyes opened. "Ah, here she is," he said. "My favorite girl child."

Mom was seated next to him, looking pretty pleased to be there. She would visibly relax the moment he hit our porch steps, and they'd gab nonstop, as if catching up on all the matters they'd left undiscussed while he was gone.

I picked up bits of their conversation as I moved from kitchen to dining room, setting the table, now and then easing my pace to catch the finer details.

"Remember what I told you about Gladys and you-know-who?" I heard Mom inquire. Dad mumbled something. "Well, he really did phone her, and she said, 'Annie, he sounds absolutely charming, not at all the way I remember him. When is he going to show himself to the rest of his old classmates?'"

She had to mean Barney. I set Danny's plate down in slow motion and tuned in my ears.

"And I said, 'Meaning you?' And Gladys said, 'Well...' Naturally I hopped on that one. 'If you'd like, Gladys,' I said, 'I can—arrange—'" Her voice hung high. "Suzy, what is taking you so long? Four plates, four glasses and silverware should not become a lifetime project."

Their talk dwindled to whispers and smothered laughter.

Danny made it home just in time to sit down and pick his way through the meal. Then, barely acknowledging us, he hopped up and washed his face and combed his hair and took off.

"If I didn't know the kid was too young for it," Dad observed, "I'd think he's suddenly 'discovered women.'"

"They're never too young," Mom said. "At least, not when that woman is Merilee Hayden, TV soap star. In fact, she seems to have infected the neighborhood with the disease. Jimmy Wingate—"

"Jimmy? Faithful old Jimmy? I find that hard to believe."

"Believe." Mom darted me a glance, then looked away. "Of course we have been running a sort of exchange student program. Jack Faraday's parked here just about every night this week. And your daughter hasn't exactly been complaining."

Dad's eyebrows shot heavenward. And Mom's lips formed the message, *We'll talk about it later.*

Later turned out to be after the dishes, while I was stashed in the entry hall with my fingers near the phone, waiting for an expected call from Jack.

It seemed at least as important to overhear what Mom was about to confide to Dad.

From a carefully selected spot near the living room, I could see Dad relight his briar and hunch forward as if listening.

"For one thing," Mom was saying, "Jack doesn't smoke, doesn't drink, is not hooked on drugs. He told me he has no intention of muddling his brain with mind-benders."

"Commendable," Dad said.

"And he's actually not locked into acting for the rest of his life. That's imitate-and-obey, like animals in a circus, he says. He wants to control, not obey."

"No crime," Dad said. He took an experimental puff.

"Jack wants to produce or direct. That's where the power is, that's the way to get ahead in the business, he went to great lengths to let us all know."

"The American way," Dad said.

Small silence. And then Mom cleared her throat. "Jack's really given me no problems, when it comes to Suzy, I'll say that for him. But..."

I stood absolutely still, wanting to hear every word.

"Why don't I like him, Bob? Why don't I trust that boy's motives?"

Dad leaned back against the cushions and delivered a wavering stream of smoke past a tiny smile. "Beats me," he said.

She had no reason, I thought. No real reason. After all, what had Jack ever done to her? Oh, maybe asked for an extra bag of pretzels, commented too acidly on one of her pet TV shows...

Well, I wouldn't let her warped prejudices influence my decisions. No way. What I did or didn't do about Jack would be up to me. Totally.

So when the phone finally rang I was on top of it, ready for whatever.

But not quite ready for that particular phone call.

Jimmy sounded a little blurred, as if a head cold had invaded his sinuses. But the message came through sharp and clear. He'd quit his extra-hours job at the Superette.

Jimmy and his Uncle Steve had exchanged heated words, and his uncle had shouted some "really unforgivable" things about Merilee. Called her, among other more colorful goodies, a hard-bitten little "actress" who was playing nasty games with the emotions of a young untried lad from the country. "That's me," Jimmy said. "Young and untried." And then he went on, "I don't care what he calls me. But—Merilee—"

"That's the way some people are." I recalled bits of an article I'd read somewhere. "They think in stereotypes. Like, *real* women stay home and cook and have babies and *real* men stalk the marketplace and bring home the bacon. And fortune-tellers and actors are performing the work of the devil. That sort of thing. And if anybody dares to disturb their precious images—"

"Hey, my Uncle Steve, to a T."

"It takes time for narrow minds to accept a new thought. In fact, this article I was reading—"

"Boy, have you nailed it down! Typical small-town thinking! I'll bet it was reasoning like my uncle's that drove Barney Stokes from town all those years ago! He made himself do what I'm going to do once I graduate. Head for the city. Yeah. The Big Apple itself, where you're not prejudged by your looks or your views, or what you do for a living. And they say the air is purer out here, huh? Shows how little we know."

"Now slow down, Jimmy, aren't you jumping to—"

"I've got you to thank, Suzy, for bringing this to my attention. It's exactly what I needed to hear. And whatever future life decisions I make will be due to what you said. You know what I mean. That business about the typical narrow minds in small towns."

"Hey, hold it! Did I say that? Because if I did—*Jimmy*?"

He'd already hung up.

"What? No male visitor from across the street tonight?" My mother sounded amused. "You mean the last bag of pretzels is safe? And I can actually watch my suspense movie?"

"Mom, lay off! Jack said they'd be rehearsing late because the first taping begins day after tomorrow. He told me he'd call."

She moved to the living room, where she checked through a curtained window for signs of life over there. "Pretty quiet," she reported past her shoulder. "Just the Armbrusters creaking their porch rockers." Pause. "But wait! I think I hear—yes, yes, a car engine! And there they are! Jack and Sam!"

Sometimes it pays to wait out her playful moods. And by the time the phone got around to ringing again, she'd turned on her show and planted herself next to Dad on the sofa, where they'd both be for the next two hours.

Speaking of moods, Jack was in a peculiar one. At first he sounded just plain glad to talk to me. "You have no idea what a relief it is to shoot the breeze with somebody normal," he said. "You're a real joy, after the battles I've had with the supercharged personality kid I've been exposed to all day."

"Well, gee, thanks," I said.

"I like my women low-keyed and good-natured, not jabbing at me with every other breath. And I go for girls who really appreciate me, who respect my opinions, who don't put constant pressure on me to change. Suzy Jensen, I'll say it now. You're my kind of girl."

I'd been waiting for weeks to hear Jack Faraday say that. *You're my kind of girl, Suzy Jensen.* I repeated it inside my head, needing to savor the taste.

"You'll never believe the gall of that female." Jack was still talking. "They'd already set up the scene, see? With me...I mean, Kevin, in that decrepit attic, snoozing on a bunch of rags. Kevin is exhausted and gabbing in his sleep. And as the camera closes in, he mutters—well, what he mutters never gets off the drawing board. Because charming little Merilee has got the ear of the dialogue writers, and next thing I know, they've consulted with Mavis, there's a loud discussion during which Mavis is won over, and the scene is totally changed. Now, Jessica Morgan is stumbling through the brush. She tries to reach the steps of the desolate old mansion, but she falls to her knees right there in the gravel. And as the scene fades she's moaning, that heart-rending little sound that only Merilee Hayden can bring off. She thinks. If you get my point."

It did seem that an incredibly large part of my evening had been wasted on listening to one guy or the other rave about Merilee Hayden.

Chapter Ten

I phoned Jimmy. "Do you realize how long it's been since we've knocked around together on a Saturday? What say you and I explore the possibilities?"

"Hey, Suzy, ordinarily I'd jump at the chance, you know that. But Barney called to say they were making some last-minute changes in the lighting and since Sam didn't feel up to helping, would I be available. And then, when Merilee said she'd be there, too, checking out the new script, naturally I agreed to—"

"Naturally."

"Why don't you check with the other guys? Especially Jack. I'll bet *he'd* explore possibilities.... On second thought, Sam would be safer. Jack...well, I don't know about him. His intentions—"

"Are at least as honorable as Merilee Hayden's."

"What's biting you, Suzy? Look, maybe I'll call Barney back and tell him nay. Then we'll wheel out to the cove, bring our lunches, swim in the river, catch up on our chatter. Like old times. I'm sure Merilee will understand. In fact, I'd say she's one of the most understanding—"

"Don't bother."

"No bother. I'll just—"

I replaced the receiver in its hook.

Jack. I concentrated on him for an instant, picturing the auburn hair, those eyes, the lips, the sweep of jawline, waiting for that familiar tingly feeling to wash over me.

Why not go over there and meet Jack in his own territory? We could kick around a few fun ideas, and I'd let him hold my hand, and we'd hike along the riverbank and watch the trout jump, and we'd play that pick-apart game with daisies and we'd talk. Both of us would talk.

But when I got to the MacAllister place it appeared all but deserted, unless you included Sam Stokes, who was huddled in a lawn chair in the backyard with a half-empty Kleenex box nearby, looking sort of frail.

"Jack?" Sam eased himself from the lawn chair as if every bone ached. "You just missed him. He's at a rehearsal that McVane called at the last minute. Should be home in an hour." He inched back down, steepled his fingers and stared through them.

"What's wrong with you?"

"Summer cold," he croaked. He reached for a Kleenex.

"Gee, I'm sorry. I mean, what with Molly coming home and all and you feeling so rotten—"

"Molly?" He sat up straight. "Coming home? When?"

"Tomorrow night."

"Are you sure? How did you find out?"

"Let's just say I have connections." Connections, as in telephone picked up in entry hall while Mom gabbed with Mrs. Fancher on kitchen extension.

Mrs. Fancher had spelled it out. "The trip to Chicago was a disaster. I asked Adam how things had gone and he said, 'Don't ask.' And when Molly got on the phone, she sounded so quiet.

"I can't remember when she's been this depressed. I suggested to her that your Suzy go with me to the airport, thinking that some girl talk would pick up her spirits. But Molly would have none of it. She prefers to sneak home and hide herself from the cruel, cruel world. I ask you, Annie, does this sound normal?"

"Oh, come on, Gladys," Mom had said. "You know Molly. I predict that a couple of days of brooding will find her so bored with solitude—is somebody listening in on another line?"

Dead silence, from me.

"Suzy? Is that you?"

I know when to hang up quietly....

"Tomorrow night," Sam repeated to himself. "Boy oh boy, when I think of how close I came to giving up..." I caught his widening grin. "Guess what," he said. "I'm suddenly feeling much better."

He handed me the Kleenex box and was out of his chair and moving like a gazelle across the back lawn.

Danny who'd been keeping tabs on Molly's return—for Sam's benefit, I'm sure—filled us in Sunday evening with a detailed report. But who cared that she had five suitcases and one overnight bag? Or that Mrs. Fancher scraped their Ford's right fender while driving into the garage? Or that Molly tripped on some broken pavement and dropped the overnight bag, spilling its contents? What I wanted to know was—

"Did she look...oh, cheerful? Or sort of *down*?"

"It was hard to tell. I gave Sam a signal, and he sneaked across the street and waited. Soon as she spotted us, she looked the other way and hurried up their steps. And when Sam headed over she ran to the front door as though bloodhounds were chasing her. For a minute it sounded as though she was crying or had nose snuffles or something. But—" he shrugged "—maybe I was hearing wrong."

"And Sam?"

"Took off like a shot."

I could be daring and phone her. What was the worst she might do? Burst into tears? Hang up?

"She's gone to bed," Mrs. Fancher intercepted after the first ring. "I know that doesn't sound like Molly, but she is terribly tired. Try again tomorrow, Suzy."

A rap on their front door, Monday morning, after Mrs. Fancher had left for work, produced total deadening silence.

"Seems to me," Jimmy volunteered as we started our trek to Stokeses', "that Molly needs time to recuperate. Maybe a little less pressure from her friends would help."

We stopped at his house to pick up some stuff. While I waited in the Chevette, Camille limped along their driveway, then draped herself onto the lawn. She crossed her front paws and stared morosely past them. She spotted me. From her throat came this strange wheezy noise that I took for a bark of welcome. Her tail thumped, swayed uncertainly, then drooped to stillness. Her head slid farther onto the paws and settled there.

Jimmy careened down the porch steps, spied Camille and veered in her directon. He gave her a quick hug and roughed up her fur. She paid him back with a tongue lick at his ankle, then closed her eyes, as if dismissing him from her sight.

"I've seen healthier-looking specimens," I remarked.

"So have I. My mother figures it's her age; she's gradually going downhill. Mom did say she'd call the vet. Maybe a little tonic..." He climbed into the driver's seat. "Although, as Merilee says, Camille's been pretty spoiled by all the attention we've heaped on her over the years, and it could be she's just sulking. Dogs do sulk," he said, eyeing me. "They're a lot like little kids, when the spotlight's been turned onto somebody else." He brushed at the blondish fuzz sprouting beneath his nose and turned on the ignition. "At least, that's what Merilee says."

The first taping was set for that afternoon. After a quickie lunch of pickle loaf sandwiches and something wet to wash them down, they did a run-through with the director, the actors and the technical crews. Everybody pounced in with suggestions for changes. For a while things got pretty hairy. A full dress rehearsal followed and some last-minute cuts in dialogue and action. Taping was scheduled for two-thirty.

Immediately after lunch the sky clouded up and I thought, Oh, no! If it rains, they'll have to cancel. But McVane said, "Perfect! Exactly what we need for atmosphere," and rubbed his palms together as if he'd just been awarded a prize.

I'll say now, it was an *experience*. I mean, everything meshed together so beautifully! As if Jessica and Josh and Kevin had been secretly stashed inside of three actors' bodies, and when two-thirty arrived and the cameras started to roll, they exploded to life. And to add to the feeling of mystery, while they were shooting Kevin's scene, the clouds darkened and the raindrops came, drizzling, blurring all. Then with the last take and the fade-out, the *Days of Loving* characters melted back into limbo, and Merilee, Richard and Jack emerged, real and alive and familiar. They called it professionalism. I call it magic.

Danny had come from a first-floor phone with a message for Jimmy, who was knee-deep in lighting equipment and preparing for the next day's shooting. "Your mother called," he reported. "Said to tell you the vet got there too late. Camille died at noon."

Silence.

"Your mother said, no hurry, there's nothing you can do about it now."

"Danny?" Merilee's best musical tone cut in.

Danny leaped to instant attention.

"Oh, Danny dear, may I beg a tiny favor of you?"

"Anything!" Danny's voice shrilled to a squeak. "Just ask."

Jimmy was still standing there with his face making rubbery grimaces. "M-maybe I'll go."

"A small cola, please?"

A scramble, during which Danny moved to comply and Jimmy just plain moved. Blindly. Almost knocking Barney Stokes down, in his need to get out of there.

"What's the matter with him?" Barney asked

"His dog," I said. "Camille. She died."

I guessed Jimmy went to the rest room first, because I could hear drainpipes emptying several times before finally dying away. Then I figured he probably headed for the rehearsal hall, because that was where Merilee and her cola had gone. I waited until something inside me would allow me to wait no longer, then I quietly let myself in.

From the far side of the hall, I heard voices. One was loud and hoarse. "All right. I know we all gotta go sooner or later. But it still hurts. And if you can't understand ... that ..." Jimmy's voice cracked.

Merilee's came through sweetly reasonable. "But, Jamie, she was just a *dog*. An *old* dog. It's not as if she were a member of your ... immediate family...."

There was a strangled sound from Jimmy that I interpreted as a cry of pure anguish.

"Oh, come on, calm down. I do have an idea." Her voice brightened. "My cousin Rachel's pedigreed miniature collie recently had a litter of pups, darling well-bred little things and worth a small fortune once they're registered. Now if I approach her diplomatically, she may part with one at a sensible price. And if you need a short-term loan to float it, Jamie, I'll gladly—"

"Forget it!"

Sensing a lightning exit, I slid behind the rehearsal hall door.

Jimmy, his face beet red, that ridiculous blond upper-lip fuzz quivering, loped past my hiding place and through the open front door. Once beyond the borders he broke into a run.

I eased from my sanctuary.

While I watched, Merilee idled a glance toward the window. "Oh, well," she said, shrugging. She picked up a copy of the next day's script. Her forefinger moved down a page, settling near the middle. She strode to center stage. "Kevin," she said, her voice

picking up Jessica's breathless rhythm, "you can't tell
my father—he'd never forgive me! Let me stay,
Kevin...." She started over, this time settling into
Jessica's quavery tone, "Kevin, you...can't tell my
father...he'd never...forgive..."

I quietly let myself out and caught a ride home with
Barney.

I didn't stick around our house. I knew where I had
to go.

Jimmy was in their garage, aiming a flashlight here
and there while he rummaged through some clutter.
His face has this totally beaten look, as if he'd been
awake since the beginning of time. When his fingers
reached high and latched on to a crate, the oversized
knuckles gleamed palely in the circle of light.

He turned quickly, which was when I noticed that
the blond fuzz was gone. "Oh, hi, Suzy. I see you got
home okay." A pause, while he breathed. Then he
said, "You heard about—"

"Camille? Don't you remember? I was standing
right there, when Danny... Yeah, I heard."

"I tried to find you before I left, honest I did. I'd
planned on being the first to tell you, because...well...just because." His gaze wandered to
the crate. "Figured I'd use this. For the...*you* know.
Burial."

The crate had held Jimmy's ten-speed, bought un-
assembled the summer he was twelve, and I, eleven
plus. I'd helped him assemble it. Meaning, I'd stood
by and handed him the bolts and wrenches while he'd

performed the miracle of putting together his long-awaited set of wheels. Camille had stood by, too, her button-bright eyes following every move.

We buried Camille later that evening, on a soft-earthed knoll beneath some shade trees in his Uncle Elton's back pasture. We stood together in a drizzly rain, our fingers touching, neither of us saying a word.

For once in my life I appreciated the rain splattering, dampening, making soggy streamlets down our cheeks. I mean, if anyone there had been crying, who would be able to tell?

Chapter Eleven

The next morning Jimmy came over earlier than usual. Seven-thirty, more or less. I was still bumbling to and from the bathroom, yawning, stretching, knuckling the sleep from my eyes.

Mom automatically set another place at the breakfast table, cracked open four more eggs and peeled off several slices of bacon.

"I shouldn't," Jimmy said, not really meaning it. He sat down across from me and unfolded a napkin.

He looked slightly puffy eyed, as if he'd put in a long night. There was a definite set to his lips. When he stared back at me I could see something unfamiliar brewing there.

He waited until my mother left the room for the few minutes it takes her to set out the clothes she wears when she picks up her CPA paperwork.

"About Merilee," he said. "It's true that she didn't understand about Camille and me." He dissected the bacon and combined it with an egg. "But that's just because we don't know each other well enough to pick up on every vibration. What I'm saying is, we haven't put in the years of toughing it out together that you and I have."

True. Oh how true.

"I believe that given time and effort, Merilee and I could make our own special music together. It's certainly worth a try. Because she's a great girl, Suzy. She really is."

He paused with fork in air, waiting for a comment from me. I concentrated on my orange juice, sipping it extra slowly, needing to fill my mouth with anything but words.

"I'm not going to let what she and I have been building disintegrate into just another summer romance. I'll find a way to keep in touch. And when I finally finish up here and graduation is over, and it's time to move on—"

"You'll move to the Big Apple."

"Exactly." He surveyed my plate. His eyes narrowed. "One skinny piece of toast and a blob of cottage cheese?" He hooted. "That wouldn't nourish a half-starved chicken!"

My mother had returned to her station at the kitchen range. "Try a fried egg," she coaxed. "And a lit-tle teeny slice of bacon."

I let her add the egg, not even protesting when she followed it with this double-thick bacon strip. I poked at the egg with my fork, headed it mouthward, set it down. I couldn't believe I'd actually lost my appetite. It had never happened before.

Two pairs of eyes were riveted on me.

"Something has to be wrong with her," Jimmy stated.

Mom frowned at her spatula.

"You do look kind of pale." Jimmy gazed intently at me. "Maybe you should stay home, take it a little easy. Hey, no problem. I'll explain it to Barney and the others."

"But I wanted to watch——"

"So you miss today's taping. All that's supposed to happen is, Jessica wanders into the mansion and discovers Kevin and Josh closes in on both of them. Not a big climax scene. That's scheduled for next week."

"Yeah, but..."

"I'd say play it safe, recuperate today, and tomorrow you'll be your normal bright-eyed bushy-tailed self." He patted my shoulder and mustered his "chins up" grin.

I sat before the glop on my plate and watched Jimmy leave.

"I'd say she was depressed," my mother announced to the kitchen air. "Imagine. A young girl with her whole life ahead of her, depressed. It's almost sinful." She watched me pick at the tablecloth. "Whoever said that growing up was supposed to be a ball?" Her words fell quietly between us.

"We've all reached out for an old familiar prop, only to have it fall apart in our hands. Believe me, I know how that can hurt. But the truth is, people change, feelings change. And if Jimmy..." She caught my eye. "Well, look at me," she said. "Back on my lecture circuit."

I waited for her to exit. But no such luck.

"The sad part is, Jimmy's in line for a few scars he hasn't planned on. Right now Merilee views him as an idealized image. 'Ye all-American country boy,' come to life. She'll leave here in a few days, and he'll be just another name, somebody she'd met and forgotten. And when Jimmy realizes that..."

I didn't want to hear it.

"Then of course we have Jack Faraday. He certainly has been attentive. But if you're counting on any kind of commitment..."

I got up awkwardly, knocking over my chair. I didn't stick around to set it upright.

Yesterday's rain clouds had gone on their way. Blobs of feathery white stuff now billowed against a blue-blue morning sky. The air felt squeaky clean and warm and soft as a baby's blanket. It was one of those days that sometimes shows up in mid-August and makes the rest of the month livable.

I wandered along the garden rows, snapping off a green bean and munching it, checking out a cherry tomato for ripeness. Just browsing, you could call it. Garden noises are low-key, undemanding. The whine of a honeybee doing his thing with an acorn squash blossom. The far-off warbling of wild birds. The rattle of dried peas on their withered vines when a breeze picks up and flutters them.

"Su-zy? Are you anywhere near the garden? I can really use a mess of green beans for supper!"

Okay. Okay. But I do have plans of my own, places to go, things to do—

"By all means," Mom said, "feel free to go."

Which brought me to Floyd Avenue, with my thumb pressed to the Fancher doorbell.

Molly answered the door. She didn't seem all that pleased to see me. "Well, since you're here, come on in. Grab a chair. Any chair." Ever the gracious hostess.

I cut the silence with a polite, "And how was your trip?"

"I don't want to talk about it!"

"So okay, we won't—"

"Daddy didn't want me there at all. He tried to hide it, but I could tell. And his wife is an absolute witch!"

Was she going to cry?

"Maybe she'd fooled him into thinking she accepted me, but she wasn't fooling me. I saw those glares, when she thought nobody was watching. And that so-called accident she arranged. Catching my

finger in the car door. Naturally, sweet Della denied
any guilt. She about knocked herself out apologizing
and being so sympathetic and helpful—the phony."
Molly took a ragged breath. "Daddy says he loves me.
But how come he took her side?"

"Come on, Molly, she caught your finger in the car
door on purpose? Aren't you exaggerating?"

"Well . . . it could have happened on purpose." She
glanced up. "But you want to know something that's
practically a fact? One night, while we were all sitting
around, it leaked out. Della thinks she's expecting a
baby. Daddy-O's baby. 'A little miracle child that will
cement our marriage,'" Molly mimicked. "If that's
true, I mean, if a little child will do that for a marriage, how come Daddy and my mother didn't..." She
managed a crooked smile. "I guess that pretty much
says it. I'm not miracle material."

We stared at each other for a long thoughtful moment. Then she said, "Let's get out of here."

We took a weather-beaten trail—a one-lane, wind-
ing path that eventually led to the Middle School,
where we'd both spent many lively years.

After a while we found ourselves edging the long-
abandoned elementary playground at the more dilap-
idated end of the school. For a time we just stood
there, kind of quiet, staring at nothing special. Then
my eyes caught the glint of sun on burnished metal. I
watched the horizontal slat suspended by chain links,
making gentle to-and-fros in the pre-noon breeze.

In the distance I could see the new playground, with its modern plastic swing seats, the giant slide with the climbing tower, the Whirly Bird, the fancy trapezes. Some other grade-school kids' fun, not ours.

"How long has it been?" Molly asked.

"Too long," I said.

And, like one, we made a leap for our old swings.

I gave a mighty backward heave that sent me soaring forward and into the air. Molly matched my pace. We hung there for one glorious instant, then settled back to earth.

Molly removed her fingers from the chains and wiped off gobs of rust. "Am I getting picky in my old age, or do these links seem a little fragile?"

I rearranged myself on the metal seat and felt the slat list to one side. An ominous creaking accompanied it. Why did I get the feeling those swings were trying to tell us something?

We moved to a nearby curb and sat down. "Everything I touch these days goes sour," she said, hugging her knees and looking glum. "Suzy, what's the matter with me?"

I searched my brain for a wise, uplifting answer. Nothing came.

"Take that thing with Jack," she went on. "I was so sure he and I would . . ." She darted me a glance. "My mother says you've been making time with him. Is she right?"

"Well . . ."

"And you're actually making inroads? I wish you all kinds of luck."

"Gee, thanks."

"Oh, you needn't feel guilty on my account. I've given it lots of thought, and my eyes are wide open about him now. The way I see it, take away Faraday's eyes and hair, his smile and the rest of that gorgeous, gorgeous body—" she inhaled, then carefully exhaled "—I mean, take them away, and what have you got? Just another male. No better, no worse than your average male here in Hillsboro. Right?"

What could I say?

"No better, no worse than, say, Jimmy Wingate. With one important difference. Jack will be attentive and charming, then he'll tire of you, and poof! he's off chasing another butterfly. Whereas, Jimmy, being the constant, loyal person we all know he is, will be around, and yours, forever."

Apparently Molly's mother hadn't clued her in on *every*thing.

"Hey, there are other guys available, Molly. In fact, I know of one very nice guy who's dying to ask you out."

She sat up straight. "No way. I'm giving up all that, Suzy. I have in mind more serious matters. Like, what to do with the rest of my life. Like, what good I can do for the world's less fortunate. Like, how I can best utilize my talents."

"And?"

"I'm thinking, *nun*, right now. And, *convent*. Yeah. Isolated convent in, say, the undeveloped back hills of Alaska."

"It would help if you were Catholic."

"Oh. Yes. Well, that's one of the unresolved parts I'm giving deep thought to." Her voice died away. She closed her eyes.

"Just in case you're interested, the boy's name is . . ."

She opened her eyes.

"Sam. As in Stokes."

"Sam Stokes?" She caught my eye. "Sam is . . . nice," she acknowledged. "But hardly my type."

"You have a type?"

"Sam," she repeated, as if tasting the name. She shrugged. "Oh, maybe someday, when I'm more into that sort of stuff."

"Well, 'someday' had better get with it, because the *Days of Loving* gang will be leaving Hillsboro in a very few days."

Silence, during which she picked at her fingernails. "To tell you the truth," she said finally, "I'm a little gun-shy. I mean, after what happened with Jack." Her gaze wandered, then settled on the now-motionless swings. She stood up. "Let's get out of here. This place gives me the creeps!"

At the supper table that night we heard the news. There was to be a party, given by Mom and Dad, a get-together of their high school ex-classmates still living in the area.

"Nothing excessive," Mom promised. "A family affair, picnic-style on the back lawn, with the kids helping to set up and clean up." She consulted her list and added a couple of names.

"You think I don't know what you're up to?" This, from Dad, grinning over the top of the *Fleet City Evening Star.*

Mom glanced up from her list.

"You're dying to show Barney off to all those wonderful folks who wrote him off as a nothing, back when. And," he said, flipping to the sports page, "it wouldn't surprise me if you planned to rub a few arrogant noses in it."

"Why, Bob, such a thing to say!"

"Not only that," he added, looking extra wise, "it wouldn't amaze me if you were up to some devilment again!" He went back to the sports page, but I could see he was still grinning.

"You say this picnic is slated for Wednesday?" Danny piped up. "Maybe you shouldn't count on me. Chances are, I'll be pretty busy that night, doing my own thing."

"I have news for you," Mom said coolly. "Chances are, you'll be doing nothing else, that night. You'll be here, helping, right along with everybody else."

"We can probably get Molly," I said. "I'll ask her anyway."

"By all means, ask Molly," Mom said. "She may be just the catalyst we need, to—" She broke off to sneak a look at Dad. "Then there's Sam, who'll naturally be invited right along with Barney. Such a nice boy. I'm sure he'll be glad to help. And of course," she said, "we'll need Jimmy."

"Don't count on Jimmy," I advised her. "He's not exactly with it these days."

"I'm counting on him. Period."

My mother, the optimist. Well, at least I'd warned her.

Chapter Twelve

Thursday's taping was to be the "big clinch" scene, the delicious, long-awaited moment in which Kevin and Jessica finally discover each other. I mean, *discover*. As in: faces meet, lips touch, arms wrap around, bodies draw close.

"If you think I'm thrilled about it," Jack sounded off to me, "think again. I'd rather kiss an alligator."

"The sacrifices one must make for one's career," I drawled. "Poor fellow."

We were in the living room, huddled on a love seat and watching a vintage movie on the TV. Jack was putting away his usual pistachio-mint ice cream, while I concentrated on strips of raw carrot and rings of green pepper. I was trying to convince myself it takes time to develop a love for the stuff.

"Of course, Jimmy, being kind of dumb about such matters, has to confuse acting with real life. He's so sure that once we touch, Merilee and I will be swept by wild passion and I'll carry her off to my castle." Jack sprinkled some nuts on the pistachio mint. "Ever since he heard about Thursday's taping, he's been hovering over Merilee like a white knight sworn to protect ye innocent young maiden from the unspeakable. Man, how that guy can hover!"

"Jimmy Wingate's specialty," I said, keeping it light. I bit down hard on a carrot, catching my lower lip, drawing blood, which I wiped with the back of my hand.

Jack examined my hatchet job. "Hey, I'll bet that really hurts," he said.

There must have been pain. I mean, why else would my eyes fill with sudden tears? And why the bitter taste in my mouth?

"I have the perfect cure." Jack smiled, showing all of his canine teeth. He leaned into me, covering my lips, injury and all, with his own.

I would like to report that it did wonders for my pain. But a few minutes of Jack Faraday's idea of therapeutic kissing could be more than enough. He'd gone at it in an entirely different way. With unexpected energy. And expertise. As if he'd been operating at half throttle until then and now the kid gloves were off. I hesitate to admit it, but I was tremendously relieved when my dad came in and made loud harrumphy noises that made Jack pull away.

The funny part is, in my daydreams that was exactly how he would kiss me. Urgently, with insistence, promising knee-trembling moments of pure pleasure. I guess you could say I'm very good at daydreaming.

Jack smoothed back his hair. "Sorry about that, Suzy," he said, looking contrite. "Hope I didn't cause more damage."

No damage that wouldn't heal. Call it a learning experience. I'd got the definite impression that Jack hadn't really been kissing me, Suzy Jensen; he'd been marking time filling in with a girl who happened to be me until the real one came along.

Thursday's taping brought a couple of us members of the viewing public onto the *Days of Loving* scene.

Of course I'd received a special go-ahead from Jack. "What? You're that eager to watch Kevin Dowling have his way with the dainty Jessica? Well, why not? Take notes. A little education on your part might do us both a world of good, if you get what I mean, haha." And I'd preyed on Molly's natural curiosity about Merilee, using my diplomatic skills to lure her to come with me.

She and I used our faithful old ten-speeds, showing up shortly before the run-through rehearsal.

Everybody there seemed totally engrossed. The actors had drifted to private corners of the "big clinch" set and were silently mouthing lines, plus now and then eyeing their blocked-out floor positions. Jimmy and Sam were hauling unwieldly sections of lighting equipment past endless coils of black cable, while trying to avoid getting conked by the microphones of the snakelike sound "booms."

I could pinpoint the exact instant that Sam spotted Molly, that disastrous moment when his feet got caught in the black coils, his forehead cracked against the mike, and down he crashed to the floor.

For once Molly had enough sense not to laugh. She actually had enough class to look elsewhere while he picked himself up and wiped at his flushed face.

I steered her to an exit. We wandered to the bird-bath area and refreshed ourselves with some cola and leftover sandwiches, just like in the old days.

Molly was full of talk about Merilee. "My gosh, she is gorgeous," she enthused. "Did you notice her skin? And those lashes! The hair! That figure!" She leaned close to me. "I don't want to ruin your day, Suzy, but I couldn't help noticing...well, Jimmy... Did you see the way he looked at her? As if she were some goddess, for heaven's sake!"

As if on cue, Merilee strolled in our direction. She acknowledged our presence with a half smile, then hied herself off to someone seated behind the bird-bath.

"Aunt Shelley!" Merilee sounded genuinely surprised. "What brings you out here?"

A skinny middle-aged person with orange hair hopped up and embraced her. "My dear, I simply could not resist watching this particular taping. You know how I feel about that young man." She pursed her lips. "All right, laugh, if you will, about my hunches. But I'm rarely wrong about these things. And I'll say it again, today you and he—"

"Have some cola, Aunt Shelley," Merilee cut in. "And I do believe there is one brownie left. Here. Take it. Please."

"Mer-i-*lee*," Barney called from the doorway. "Time for the run-through!"

Molly and I stayed outside during the run-through, sipping soft drinks and rattling on about unimportant things. For her sake we kept it that way. Low-key and unemotional. Besides, I was saving my main strength for the dress rehearsal. As Jack had put it, that would prove most educational.

Merilee's Aunt Shelley seemed content to stay where she was. After a while she slapped on a pair of granny glasses, picked a paperback from her tote bag and began to read.

Danny came out and said, "Guess what? They're doing the dress rehearsal!" Molly and I came to life and moved with galloping speed. Aunt Shelley dumped the paperback and granny glasses into her tote bag and sprinted inches behind us. We made it to the "big clinch" set in a dead heat.

Jimmy sat beneath a klieg light, elbows resting lightly on knees, hands dangling, looking relaxed, yet alert, the perfect image of an apprentice lighting technician following the action. But I could see the muscles tighten in his neck, and as Jessica reached out a slender hand to Kevin I caught the watchful expression on his face.

"Boy, am I glad those two hate each other," Danny muttered. "Because if they didn't..." The corners of his mouth turned down.

Gerard McVane was perched on a nearby canvasback chair, running a finger down the lines of the TV script, sometimes making notes in a huge steno pad, sometimes barking out instructions. Barney had secluded himself and his copy of the script in a shadowed corner. He smiled a welcome to Molly when we came in, then returned to brooding concentration.

"Now move in closer," McVane directed. "Kevin, take Jessica's hand and... Kevin?"

Jack glared, then reached forward, grabbing at Merilee's hand the way you'd grab at an electric fence.

Merilee pressed her lips together and pulled away.

McVane whacked his knuckles against his forehead. "Ye gods, can't you two bury the hatchet long enought to—"

"All *right*." Jack seized Merilee's shoulders, hauling her to him. He pushed his face skin-close to hers, and his mouth against her mouth.

There was a space during which everybody sort of held one long breath. From the corner of my eye I could see Jimmy slide down in his chair and close his eyes.

"Well." McVane had resumed breathing. "Fine." He rubbed his palms together. "Now that's what I call professionalism." Another space. "Okay, kids, you can break it up now."

Only, they weren't breaking it up.

"Hey!" Danny swiveled his sights to Barney. "What's the matter with those guys?"

Barney set down the script copy and folded his arms. "I dunno," he said.

"I told her so!" This, from Aunt Shelley, who had jumped to her feet and was marching around, swinging her tote bag. "I told her this would happen."

"Huh!" From behind Molly's hand. "He never kissed me that way."

"Maybe it's catching," Sam murmured. He was looking at Molly.

Jack and Merilee came apart reluctantly. They started at each other. "Wow," he said softly. Merilee's face was glowing. She reached up and patted his cheek. "That was just wonderful," she said. And they closed ranks again, kissing as if time and audience no longer mattered.

Chapter Thirteen

Jimmy wouldn't come out of the house. I knew that, because when I tossed a pebble at his bedroom window with its shade half-drawn, a large-knuckled hand abruptly yanked the shade all the way down. And when I called there after arriving home, he wouldn't answer the phone.

"I'm sorry, Suzy," Mrs. Wingate said, "he's...well, indisposed. Maybe later."

Molly came over around five. "You should have stayed," she said. "The taping went beautifully."

"So glad," I muttered.

"They really do look darling together. And so happy. You know, the funny part is, I don't feel all that bad about it. Of course, you..." She flashed me a sympathetic glance. She cradled her knees and looked at me through her lashes. "Tell me for a fact, Suzy, did it bother you? I mean, did you feel as totaled out as I did when—"

"I felt relief. And that's a fact."

"Oh, sure."

It was true. The instant I saw them kiss, it was as if a giant weight had fallen from me. I think I realized then, that although I didn't hate Jack Faraday, I didn't particularly like him, either. And I knew, finally, that it was *Kevin Dowling* who had caught my fancy— *Kevin*, who had raced the blood through my veins.

I don't know why it had taken me so long to get it through my head that although Kevin and Jack might be sharing the same outside shell, and Jack could, on cue, fool a person into believing he was this macho character named Kevin, the resemblance stopped there. Kevin Dowling, human being, did not exist. He was a creation of the *Days of Loving* writers, the producers, the directors, the camera crew, the audio and lighting crews, the makeup department and an actor's ability. A manufactured product.

"I'll admit it did help to have Sam there," she said. "We talked for quite a while, after the taping. He's really a very sweet guy, Suzy, did you know that? But then," she added, looking thoughtful, "you probably did. Anyway, he's asked me out, and I'm going. I'm taking it slow and easy this time. Testing the water, you might say. If I read the vibrations right, Sam

Stokes and I will stay in touch. And if loving a person has anything to do with liking him first, who knows?''

With Molly, you could only hope. Part of me had to be rooting for both of them. But most of me was closeted in that darkened room in the Wingate house, hurting along with Jimmy.

As for Danny, he had just suffered through his first jolting discovery: that the princess was a commoner after all. But my kid brother was like a rubber ball; he'd bounce back.

With Jimmy, it ran deeper. He'd made plans—life plans—twisting them to fit a future that he'd been so certain would include Merilee Hayden.

Mrs. Wingate came over after supper. She accepted a cup of coffee and a slice of raisin and nut bread. "Jimmy's really down about this," she told Mom and me. "Charlie and I were fully prepared to let him work it out himself. Give it a little time and water under the bridge. That's how we handled it when Paul and Elinor were his age." She stirred a spoon in her coffee. "Then Barney Stokes phoned and offered to see the boy. I asked him why and he said, 'I've been there, I understand what he's going through. Sometimes it helps to have a person around who will just sit there and listen.'" She eyed Mom. "Does that make sense to you?"

"Listening?" Mom pursed her lips. "Of course I'm no expert, but they do say that listening is good therapy."

"Anyway, he came over. It did do a little. At least Jimmy came downstairs, and that's an improvement."

I had to put in a word. "Mrs. Wingate, would it help if I talked to him?" She turned to look at me. "Sometimes kids find it easier to talk to other kids—if you know what I mean."

"Suzy, why don't we leave it at this? I'll broach the subject to Jimmy, and we'll see what happens. All right?"

A half hour later he called.

He sounded like Jimmy, only flat, as if a giant steamroller had gone over his voice. "I just thought I'd tell you, I'm going away for a few days, to my brother Paul's in Baltimore."

Going away. It had such a mournful ring. Like the clang of funeral bells.

"I gotta sort things out. Make sense of...you know. What's real." I waited out the pause. "Figured I'd tell you first, because we've gone through so much together. I mean, we're friends, Suzy. Right?"

I tested for voice and found one. "Right."

"Barney suggested it. He said the change in perspective would help. So Mom called Paul and he said, 'Sure, send the kid out. Mary and I'll show him the bright lights of Baltimore and introduce him to some wild, wild women.'" Jimmy's laughter was a puny little sound from the back of his throat. "This, as we all know, is what I really need right now. A few wild, wild women." The laughter trickled to silence.

"It'll do you a world of good to get away from this town!" I chirped. "New experiences, new people, isn't that supposed to be the cure-all for just about anything? As for that rotten business of Merilee and Jack..."

"Hey, *drop* it!"

"I only meant—"

"Look, I gotta go now. I'll phone you from Baltimore, Suzy, first chance I get. Okay?"

On Tuesday, shortly after the ten-o'clock news on TV, the call from Baltimore came.

"Suzy? Can you hear me? Guess who this is."

"It has to be my old buddy, J. T. Wingate. And, yes, I can hear you just fine."

"Aha," he said, "you remember me."

"How could I forget?"

He laughed as if I'd said something very witty. "Well, it's nice to hear that, anyway." I could make out a bass voice sounding off in the background. Probably Paul's. "What I wanted to tell you is, I'm coming home tomorrow. Will you call my mother and let her know?"

Hey! He'd actually phoned me before contacting his own mother!

"Tell her I tried to get her earlier, but the connection was so poor... Suzy? You still there?"

"Yup."

"And tell her that Paul's wife, Mary, is putting me on the plane, and I'll call her when I got to the airport."

"Right, old buddy."

"One more thing. Remember that problem I had, back there in Hillsboro? The one with . . . with the actors? Well, I've been giving it plenty of thought, and I've come to some conclusions about—"

"For crying out loud, Jim! I thought you said you'd keep the call short."

"Oh. Yeah. Okay, Paul. Well, good night, Suzy. See you sometime tomorrow."

See you sometime tomorrow had to be the sweetest words I'd heard in a long time.

Chapter Fourteen

The reunion party was scheduled for eight the next evening. Dad had set out the tables and lighting, and made a macaroni salad and the whipped gelatin, and sliced the roast beef and ham. The rest of it was left to Mom and me and whomever we could con into helping.

Mrs. Fancher, with Molly in tow, showed up at our house at ten in the a.m., armed with a sack of potatoes and a paring knife. After a few minutes of diligent peeling, she handed the knife and the rest of the spuds to Molly, then sat herself down and imbibed coffee while she and Mom gabbed.

I hung out with Molly, until Sam arrived and planted himself in our living room. The last I saw of them, they were sitting on the love seat, watching a game show on TV. The sack and knife lay on the coffee table but Molly and Sam were obviously too busy watching to pay attention to me. So back to the kitchen and my old enemies, caked-over pots and pans.

I kept the sounds of scouring down to a whisper. It seemed the only way to stay out of the limelight and at the same time to monitor the coffee-break conversation. And an illuminating conversation it turned out to be.

"I saw Barney in town yesterday," Mrs. Fancher was saying between bites of marmalade on muffin. "My-o-my, hasn't he matured gracefully! He waved when he saw me, but I got the feeling he preferred not to visit."

"To the contrary," Mom said, spreading apple butter on her toast. "Barney would love to—"

"I'd definitely say he's avoiding speaking to me," Mrs. Fancher cut back in. "Yes, except for that one phone call, I'm like paper on the wall to Barney Stokes. It certainly is deflating. What I'd like to know, Annie, is why? What have I ever done to him?"

"You don't understand, Gladys. Barney feels very strongly about—"

"Back then I did tease him a lot," Mrs. Fancher allowed. "I just couldn't resist it. He'd blush and stammer and stare at the ceiling, and I'd keep right on teasing. Adam used to say that Barney had a crush on me, and if I didn't take it easy on the poor boy, he'd get ideas. But I really don't . . . think . . ." She bit into the muffin.

"Who knows what really goes on in the head of a teenage boy?" Who indeed, I silently concurred.

"I don't know if you realize what a practical joker Adam could be. One night just before graduation he cooked up this really dumb prank, which, of course, he didn't fill me in on until years later. Anyway, he got Patsy Miller to call up Barney and pretend she was me, inviting him to a moonlight swim at the Cove. I'm sure Barney didn't buy it. For one thing, Patsy wasn't a very good impressionist. For another, Adam and I had been going steady since that Easter—; *every*body knew it, so there was no reason for Barney to assume—"

"Logical thinking," Mom said. "Why would any sensible person assume such a ridiculous thing?"

Mrs. Fancher's eyes opened wide. "He...didn't..."

"He did."

She stared at the marmalade leaking from her muffin. "At the Cove, waiting for me?"

"Until midnight. He huddled on that old stump along the shore, shivering in his bathing trunks, checking his watch every minute or so, staring into the night...."

"And then?"

"He went home, his father caught him at the front door, there was a confrontation and Barney vowed he'd leave Hillsboro and never come back again." She smiled, showing her dimple. "Which proves, I suppose, that given enough time, we all mellow."

"He must hate me," Mrs. Fancher said.

"Guess again," Mom said.

Silence, while Mrs. Fancher digested what she'd heard. Then she said, "He used to confide in you?"

"He desperately needed to talk out his problems with somebody," Mom said. "After all, who did he have? No mother, a father filled with such bitterness he scarcely acknowledged his own son... Mama would send me to the Stokes farm to buy fresh milk, and as Barney and I chatted the words would tumble out. About his loneliness, his awkward shyness around the others in our class and that wondrous invention of nature, Gladys Owens."

Mrs. Fancher's lips formed a tiny smile.

"And then one afternoon he blurted that Gladys had actually called to ask him to meet her at the Cove that night. He was so absolutely bowled over by the possibility—the first positive thing to happen to him in years. I warned him to go slow, I reminded him that you and Adam were a steady item, I even hinted at the possibility of a hoax. But he wanted so badly to believe..." Mom tested the apple butter, then set her toast down.

"He phoned me the next day. The letdown had hit, full force. Gladys had been toying with his emotions, his father had chewed him out, nothing was working out for him, nobody cared—'Nobody?' I said. 'I care. And the others would care if you'd give them half a chance to know the real you.' But he'd had it with Hillsboro, he'd..."

Water glanced off the copper-bottom pan I'd been rinsing and spritzed all around.

Mrs. Fancher ran some fingers along the back of her neck. They came away damp. "Annie," she murmured, "did I ever tell you the one about the cute pitcher with the extra-large ears?"

My mother's gaze shifted and locked with mine. "Suzy," she said, "why don't you slide downtown and get ginger ale for the punch?"

I made a rough estimate of about forty-five people as they worked from table to table, filling and refilling their paper plates with ham, roast beef, cold cuts, three kinds of salad, baked beans, the zucchini bread, cheesecake, the whipped gelatin, you name it. The kids mostly hit the fruit punch with a vengeance and the adults did likewise to a keg of beer.

The social atmosphere, at first strained, gradually thawed. By the time the ham and whipped gelatin had run out, the Hillsboro High alumni were calling each other by almost forgotten nicknames and dredging up memories of Mrs. Catlin's English Lit III class and the senior trip to Cooperstown.

Seth Thomas, college freshman son of Mr. and Mrs. Dave Thomas, had brought along a guitar and began plinking sentimental tunes from that bygone era. The remnants of the old gang chimed in, shoulder to shoulder, as the sun slid into the horizon and the string of lights rigged by my dad flicked on.

Barney was a vital part of a trio, singing harmony, belting out, in his deep voice, the lyrics to "Yesterday When I Was Young," while Dad took the baritone, and Mr. Thomas, the tenor. Mrs. Fancher whispered to Mom, from her spot behind the cheesecake, "This is the shy Barney Stokes I used to know?"

Anyone could tell that she was impressed. In fact, Barney seemed to be impressing quite a few of his ex-classmates.

"Did you see the expression on Patsy Wilcox's face?" Mom's lips curled. "There was a time she wouldn't have given him a second look."

"Isn't it sickening the way she hangs all over him?" From the back of Mrs. Fancher's hand. "Just because they're both connected with *drama*..."

"Gladys," Mom said patiently, "I'll ask you one more time. Do you or do you not want me to arrange something with Barney? I'm sure he's willing—"

"If he's that willing, then where is he?" Mrs. Fancher's spine had gone suddenly stiff. "I firmly believe it's the man's place to..." Her spine collapsed. "Oh, Annie, you know I do! But how can I? If he still thinks I stood him up, all those years ago..."

Pause, while Mom thought. Then she said, "Gladys, I just had the most fabulous idea! First, I need some answers. One: do you want to see Patsy brought down a peg or so?"

"We-e-ell."

"Two: will you let me do something really wonderful for Gladys Owens Fancher?"

"I, uh, why not?"

"Then watch."

Mrs. Wilcox was burning Barney's ears with animated conversation when my mother sauntered over. "It makes me feel so good, watching two old classmates catch each other up on the years," she cooed. She shoulder-clutched Mrs. Wilcox. "Has our Patsy told you yet, how involved she is in local drama?"

"Several times," Barney said, fingering a mug of beer.

"She was quite the comedienne as Eileen, in the spring production of *Wonderful Town.*"

"So I've been hearing." Barney downed half the contents of the mug.

"And the joy is, she's so multitalented. Sings, dances, and, would you believe...does impressions?"

"Oh?" Barney sounded more polite than interested.

"Um...not all that well, really." Mrs. Wilcox looked faintly uncomfortable. "It's been a long time, since I—"

"Ah, Patsy, you are just too modest." Mom brightened. "Remember that time, just before graduation, when you and Adam Fancher cooked up that devilish scheme to call up Barney and pretend—"

"Pretend?" Barney looked up. "What are we talking about, here?"

"It was Adam's idea," Mrs. Wilcox put in quickly. "I merely supplied the voice."

"For what?" She had Barney's full attention.

"Does it matter now?" Mrs. Wilcox glanced hurriedly past her shoulder, then back, not quite meeting his eye. "Oh, well, since the story has obviously made the rounds... Anyway, I never did believe you bought the idea. For one thing, I wasn't all that great at impressions. And then Gladys has a certain timbre to her voice that absolutely defies imitation. Still, I did what I could. And Adam said you'd be so thrilled by the possibility of moonlight-dipping with Gladys, you'd buy a gorilla, shrieking."

Barney looked thoughtful. "Swimming? At the Cove?"

"Right. Pretty tacky, huh? But that was Adam Fancher's idea of a practical joke." She held out her hands. "No hard feelings?"

He stared at her through hooded eyes. After a minute his gaze shifted to my mother. They exchanged a long look. Then Mom winked.

A tiny smile started at the creases of Barney's mouth, expanding suddenly to a full-blown grin. He grabbed hold of Mrs. Wilcox's outstretched hands and shook them. "No hard feelings!"

He loped over to the table where Mrs. Fancher stood, scooped out a large slab of cheesecake and set it on a plate. Then he poked through the plastic forks, selecting a matched pair and gathered up some napkins and two mugs of beer. "Gladys," he said, "care to join me in a little refreshment?"

It was time for me to move away and leave them to rediscover each other.

I hung around watching people I'd known all my life have such a great time and felt a little empty. There had still been no word from Jimmy.

Across Meridian, under the MacAllister porch lamp, Jack and Merilee sat—he, on the top step, she just below him. I think they were holding hands. I think Jack let go long enough to wave to me. I didn't wave back.

After a minute they got up and ambled to the beginning of our driveway doing some rubbernecking of their own.

It would be one of their last chances. Barney had mentioned earlier that the on-location stay was almost over. A few more scenes, including the big climax scene, then they'd pack up equipment, clothes and the Armbrusters and head back to the Apple.

"I wonder if they'd mind if we took a look-see," Jack said to Merilee, but loud enough for me to catch. "I mean, I've learned to love the folks in this town; they're mighty fine people, they're like *family*."

"Hear, hear," Merilee chanted, hanging on to his arm and gazing sentimentally toward the softball game.

As one of the "folks in this town" that Jack had "learned to love," I'd just as soon they didn't bother.

My mother spotted me from afar. "Suzy," she called, "how about bringing out that other platter of roast beef on the kitchen table?"

Well, why not? Anything would be better than standing around watching people have a ball while I waited for other people who never showed.

I'd just made it to the kitchen, when the phone rang.

"Hey, I'm back! Got any leftovers for a wandering pal?"

Chapter Fifteen

Jimmy met me by the punch bowl. I loaded his plate with a bit of everything that was still left, got his tableware, steered him in the direction of the front lawn and sat down next to him.

I waited for him to talk, which took practically forever, since he insisted on finishing his roast beef first. "I saw Barney and Mrs. Fancher," he commented. He set down his fork. "What is it with those two?"

How to put it? "Time, catching up...brought on by a bad joke resurfacing." His puzzled expression said that I wasn't getting through. "Okay," I said, "call it...starting over again."

"I approve of starting over again," Jimmy said. He dangled a slice of bologna over his mouth, then gobbled it whole. "Barney told me we'll be seeing a lot of him from now on. He says he'll be coming back to Hillsboro every free weekend he can squeeze in and he'll bring Sam with him when he's able to. They'll be staying at his home place, fixing it up as they go along." He poked through the macaroni and tuna salad, tested a sample, downed a clump of it. "I guess Barney finally got the news that the old hometown ain't so bad after all." He caught my eye and grinned.

I watched him eat. For once it was a pleasure. "Have you, uh, heard how the show's coming along?" he asked when his initial hunger had been somewhat satisfied.

"On schedule. They finish the final scenes on Friday. Jack, Merilee, Aunt Shelley and the Armbrusters leave on Saturday, followed by the camera and lighting equipment. Barney, Sam, Richard and what's left of the crews stick around until Sunday afternoon to clean up."

"And it'll all be over," he said.

I could feel a gap in conversation coming on. I plunged in with small-talk to fill it. "Of course Molly and I still have this running bet about who stuffed old Ben Potter's corpse in the fireplace, and I have my own suspicions about the deep, dark Morgan family secret that Jessica happened onto—"

"Hey, know what, Suzy? I couldn't care less!" He paused. "About Baltimore," he said. "Paul and Mary really went all out to show me a big time. Mary even took a day off from her cushy government job to taxi me around to just about every historical site in town. Fort McHenry National Monument," he ticked off, "U.S.S. *Constellation*, Washington Monument, Railroad Museum, two art museums... I tell you, Suzy, I am just busting with culture." He took a breath. "And then Paul carted us both to a couple of night spots you would not believe. I mean, talk about your wild, wild women..." He looked at me slant-wise but I was having none of it.

"Then Mary did some matchmaking with the daughter of their pals in the next apartment and me. Nola, her name is. One afternoon I took her to a roller rink, and we skated for what seemed hours. She's a very nice girl, red hair, sharp figure, lively as anything. Paul and Mary think she's super, and they were talking about bringing her with them, next time they come to Hillsboro, and, you know, getting something going, with me.

"What I told them was, 'Hold off, I'm not ready for that, and I may never be. I still have some options open to me back home in Hillsboro.' Paul laughed. 'Hillboro?' he said. 'Are you kidding? After everything you've seen out here, you'd settle for Hillsboro?'" Jimmy glanced over at me. "What I'm saying is, Baltimore's a beautiful city. If you go for cities. And if you go for pretty redheads named Nola."

I swallowed hard, forcing back a comment.

The night lights dappled Jimmy's face, giving it a misty glow. He moved a little closer. "How about it, Suzy? Do I still have an option open with you?"

I moved away. "You might say that this summer's been a tough education. There have been a few scars that will take a bit of time to heal."

"If you're referring to me and Merilee," Jimmy said, leaning forward, "look, I know when I've been kidding myself. I can see now that most of it was just a buildup in my mind. And it doesn't matter as much as you think. I don't look at them as scars. More like...scratches. Yeah," he said, apparently pleased with his own definition, "surface scratches. In fact," he added, warming to his subject, "if Merilee Hayden were to walk up to me this very minute, I would say..."

He stiffened beside me. His ears had caught to-and-fro murmur of two familiar voices. And tinkly laughter, followed immediately by a deep-throated chuckle.

"Hi, you two," Merilee sang out. She glanced up at Jack. They smiled that secret little smile that people in love reserve for each other.

We watched them move on, across Meridian, back to MacAllister's.

"What say we go back and raid the rest of the leftovers?" Jimmy suggested. "You fill my plate, and I'll fill yours."

It sounded like the best offer I'd had all summer.

First Love from Silhouette

DON'T MISS
THESE FOUR TITLES—
AVAILABLE
THIS MONTH . . .

THE LOOK OF EAGLES
Ann Gabhart

It took the great heart of a little black colt to help Gillie
understand that the best way of loving is not to hold on
too tight.

DAYS OF LOVING
Jean F. Capron

When a sleepy small town was selected for taping a popular
soap opera, Suzy and Molly script a few impromptu scenes
with a cute young actor.

BEHIND THE MASK
Glen Ebisch

What in heaven's name was going on in the old museum
where Katie worked? She and her buddies would just have
to investigate—even if it meant risking their lives.

MIND OVER MATTER
Miriam Morton

When Tyne's psychic skills solved a crime, no one would
believe her but Cam. How could they get the world to take
them seriously?

WATCH FOR THESE TITLES FROM FIRST LOVE COMING NEXT MONTH

A TOUCH OF MAGIC
Jeffie Ross Gordon
Sequel to A TOUCH OF GENIUS!
Cass, Paulie and Cass's swinging grandmother, Nonna, live out their more exotic fantasies while on a whirlwind visit to New York.

TAKE A WALK
Beverly Sommers
Blythe's weird compulsion to walk out of her classes without asking anyone puzzled her teachers and parents as much as it did her. But how could she fight her own destiny—especially when it meant meeting Darwin?

DIAMOND IN THE ROUGH
Joyce McGill
Blair's friendship with the neighborhood street people involved her in some rather unsavory crimes. If they hadn't all pulled together, they might have been in deep trouble.

CASTLES IN SPAIN
Janice Harrell
When Cassie takes on an unusual commission to help finance her longed-for trip to Spain, she finds her journey fraught with complications. Fortunately, these are not all bad.

First Love from Silhouette

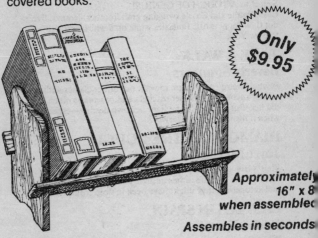